A Novel by

Vincent & Sharahnne Gibbons

In The Shadows
Written by Vincent & Sharahnne Gibbons

Cover and Illustrations by Vincent Gibbons and Jeff Jarrett
ISBN 978-1-937118-04-04 2011©
FIRST EDITION

Printed in USA by Creative Book
Printing   of Budget Transfer Printing
& Bindery www.budgettransfer.com

In The Shadows

In The Shadows

Chapter I
Majestic Mayhem

The last snowflake of the storm descended silently upon a lone snow bank in the frozen terrain.

"I see more paw prints," the tall, skinny man said. The dark one next to him nodded in agreement.

"Those do not belong to tigers," the tracker chastised as he peered down at the huge bear tracks, "Amur's prints are much wider." He stood still for what seemed like a half an hour; only his eyes moved, darting purposefully across the wintry landscape. Then, he slowly cocked his head to one side as a grin painfully threatened to crack his wind chapped lips.

"This way," he whispered.

The two men followed; the tall one closest behind the tracker.

"Wait, did you hear that?" the dark man asked in a hushed whisper.

"Hear what?" the tall one grunted.

Just then, a loud earsplitting growl was unleashed. It was so deafening that the tracker remained frozen where he stood. He managed to lift his arms in an effort to break the force of the blow, but Motka's blow was one that would not be blocked.

With one swipe of his enormous paw, he had done away with the tracker. The other two men ducked behind a tree while covering their ears. Thinking quickly, and mainly of their greedy mission to capture a tiger cub for sale on the black market, the dark man surfaced from the cover of the tree for just long enough to take one shot, hitting Motka in the neck.

Meanwhile, the tall man aimed for Senya, Bohdan's mother, who was poised in a protective stance to shield her cub.

Both shots were successful and within minutes, the massive creatures lay listlessly in the snow.

"Grab the cub!!" the dark man yelled.

The tall man then began to trudge quickly through the snow. "How will we get back without him?" he asked, nodding toward the tracker's body.

"We left footprints, you idiot! Now get the cub and let's go!!!"

The tall man hurriedly snatched the terrified tiger cub who was tightly nuzzled against his fallen mother and ran after the dark man in a hasty retreat.

Once they returned to their vehicle, he shoved the cub into a cage, latched it shut and threw a blanket over it.

The penalty for poaching and illegal animal trafficking was stiff, so the poachers were forced to use back roads and secret wooded paths to remain undetected.

The terrain was brutally rugged causing the occupants of the vehicle, including the unsecured cage carrying the tiger cub to bounce and jostle throughout the vehicle's cabin.

Bohdan was terrified and the jarring ride was even more unsettling. When he wasn't thinking about his predicament, thoughts of his parents flooded his mind. He constantly reminisced about his favorite moments: wrestling with his father and the warmth of his mother's love and milk. The milk the tall man had been giving to him was cold and tasted too sweet; also, the thick padded gloves the men wore to protect themselves from his fangs and claws were too rough against his coat.

The tall man was driving now while the dark man searched for a station on the radio.
He looked up and observed, "The journey is taking too long. We need to find a shortcut. Turn down the path here. I'm ready to collect my money! We're going to be rich!"
"Yeah," the tall man chimed in, "I'm gonna buy a year's supply of bubble gum."

"What?!" the dark man asked in bewilderment.

All of a sudden, a sloshing noise shifted his focus from the conversation to their new surroundings. A large river was now before them and they had just arrived at one of its smaller banks where the water lapped at the vehicle's front tires.

"We have to cross at the most shallow point," the dark man advised.

"This vehicle is made for this; we can cross anywhere," the tall man responded confidently.

"No, back up and we'll find a safer place to cross," the dark man exclaimed.

"See that rock right there? How deep can it be?"

The tall man shifted into second gear and proceeded to drive. However, the water was deeper than he had originally thought and it began to seep into the truck. Slightly panicked, he pressed on the gas pedal too hard, causing the wheels to spin. He shifted into reverse, but the SUV would not budge. The tall man slammed his fist against the steering wheel in frustration and disbelief as he assessed the situation.

"We're stuck! We're gonna have to get out and push," conceded the tall man.

"I told you to cross at a shallower spot, idiot!"

The exchange resulted in a brief verbal spat between the two men before they exited the vehicle to attempt to push it free.

"Well, I saw the r--hey, where'd the rock go?" the tall man exclaimed.

While the men were busy mulling over what they did or didn't see, a mob of grouchy crocodiles had been awakened by the ruckus. Their eyes and snouts gradually emerged from beneath the murky surface.

As the crocs began to close in on the source of this disturbance, the biggest croc, known as Nogard—who also happened to be the leader of these prehistoric monsters— brought up the rear as usual. The moment Nogard saw the men silhouettes, his rage spurred him to swim more quickly, bullying his way to the front of the bask.

The tall man was the first to succumb to Nogard's deadly onslaught, but thinking only of his greed, the dark man grabbed the cage and tried to swim ashore.

Nogard noticed the dark man fleeing and closed in for the kill. The dark man attempted to use the cage as a shield, but Nogard swung his massive head, sending the dark man in one direction and the cage in another. The impact was so violent that it nearly crushed the cage, causing the latch to pop open and its occupant to splash into the water.

While the rest of the colony was busy dismembering and devouring the men, out of the corner of his eye, Nogard noticed a strange little cub surfacing from beneath the rapids some distance away. Tormented by the torrent, little Bohdan instinctively swam toward the shore to safety. The big croc momentarily observed the cub struggling to climb up the steep grassy embankment before returning to the aftermath of the carnage.

Once on dry ground, Bohdan had the arduous task of navigating through the dense maze of verdant, chaotic vegetation until he found cover and relative comfort in an area of tall grass where he eventually laid down to rest.

Chapter II
Malika's Secret

Early the next morning before dawn, Malika wandered off from the festivities of a recent kill. She was one of the senior lionesses of the Nomads, the largest and most dominant pride of this uncharted region. Malika was still mourning the loss of her three-week-old cubs, which had fallen victims to a vicious crocodile attack.

As she walked through the tall foliage she suddenly stumbled across a frightened, strange-looking ball of fur in the high grass. Malika was so shocked and fascinated by the appearance of this striped creature that she kept her distance for a moment. She had encountered unusual cubs before, such as cheetahs and leopards, but never before had she seen a cub with such big feet and the most eccentric pattern of streaks as this one.

Malika also noticed that the cub didn't have the smell that normally cloaks a young one that had been tended to by his or her mother.

Nevertheless, Malika's recent loss of her own cubs overcame her natural instinct to avoid the foreigner. Instead, she decided to adopt this strange but fascinating little being.

Malika gently grabbed the scruff of Bohdan's neck in her mouth and proceeded to carry him back to her large, densely covered den located at a safe distance from the main gathering grounds of her pride.

"I'll bet you're hungry little one," Malika observed as she began to nurse the young stranger.

Bohdan ignored his own apprehension of this strange adult; he was much too hungry and grateful to reject Malika's nurturing.

The nutritious milk of the lioness allowed the tiger cub to embark upon a steady recovery from his malnourished state. Within a couple of days, little Bohdan had regained enough strength to cautiously meander about his new home. The lioness was overwhelmed with emotion as the tiger cub appeared to be extraordinarily comfortable in her presence.

The bond between the two seemed to strengthen with each passing moment as though Malika was his rightful mother.

Naturally inquisitive, she probed to find out more about her newly acquired bundle of joy.

"What are you, little one?" she asked—but Bohdan didn't respond. She then placed one of her paws on her chest and stated, "I am a lioness. What are you?"

Bohdan slightly shrugged his shoulders to indicate that he didn't have an answer.

"Do you have a name?" she pressed.

Bohdan nodded his head slowly, while staring at Malika with grateful curiosity.

"My name is Malika. What's yours?"

He remained silent for a few moments before responding softly with a strong Russian accent. "My name is Bohdan."

"What a beautiful name," Malika complimented. "You speak a strange tongue. Where are you from?"

Bohdan only dropped his head to rest on his forelegs. Realizing she had solicited enough information for one day, Malika cuddled the little orphan to comfort herself as much as him.

She never would have imagined just how much he could impact her life in such a short period of time.

Several days passed without Malika participating in a major hunt. The rest of the pride believed that she was still mourning the death of her cubs and allowed her to grieve in peace—except for Catava, a younger lioness and a familiar associate. Catava was no stranger to the sorrow that Malika was experiencing. She had lost a few cubs of her own to disease, famine and the occasional enemy. The younger lioness accepted these tragedies as the norm and was curious to know why Malika, who was older and had experienced similar sadness, had such difficulty accepting her most recent losses.

Late one evening, the lionesses of the Nomads pride gathered together as usual before heading out for a major hunt. The pride methodically trotted out into the plains with Sayid, the king of the pride, and his guardians slowly bringing up the rear.

The pride was in desperate need of a large kill therefore, the king ordered every member of the pride except Malika and the young cubs to participate in the hunt. Catava began searching for Malika, but noticed that her hunting partner was absent once more. Curious and concerned, she fell back through the ranks to be temporarily excused by King Sayid so she could check on Malika while the rest of the pride continued forward.

Though Malika was King Sayid's queen, he held Catava as his most preferred concubine. Catava genuinely admired Malika for her hunting skills and mentoring, but she was envious of Malika's status as queen. King Sayid was reluctant to allow Catava to lag behind, but she persuasively reassured him that she would catch up in time for the hunt.

Catava dashed back to remind her two cubs, Faraji and Kisa, that it was extremely important for them to stay concealed in her den until she returned. Afterwards, she headed toward Malika's den, where the adopted stranger was receiving much needed TLC.

Hearing the approaching patter of Catava's paws, Malika scurried to push Bohdan to the back of the den and quiet him before she exited to greet her friend.

Malika yelled out to Catava in an attempt to slow her approach.

"I know what you are going to say. I just haven't been in the mood to hunt."

"It is tough, but you have to get over it. We need your expertise and you can't keep going without eating," responded Catava.

Annoyed, Malika fired back defensively. "That's easy for you to say. You still have your cubs!"

"Malika, that's not fair," reasoned Catava. "We both have been through this before, and yes, you probably have been through this more times, but don't pretend as if I don't know your pain, because I do."

To quell the argument, Malika attempted to placate Catava by agreeing with her.

"You're right. I'm sorry. I don't know why—."

Catava interrupted her. "Ok, ok, now that that is settled, let's get back before Sayid sends for us." "I, uh, I-I can't," stuttered Malika.

"Why not? What's the matter now, you haven't eaten in days!" With heightened suspicions, Catava impatiently tapped her front paw as she awaited Malika's next feeble excuse.

Meanwhile, little Bohdan, innocent of the perils facing him and Malika, let his curiosity get the better of him. Sensing that his surrogate mother was close by, he decided to get a quick glimpse of his new surroundings by peeping outside of the den. Unfortunately, he caught the attention of Catava.

Distracted by the movement, Catava asked in a hushed, accusatory whisper, "Malika, you have company?"

Malika quickly denied the accusation and strategically placed herself between Catava and the den's opening to obstruct her view. Catava tried to look around her, but Malika countered each move that she made. This continued for several moments until Malika conceded her attempt to create a diversion. She realized that she would not be able to keep her secret much longer.

"I'm about to show you something that you must promise to never tell."

"Come now. You know me," reassured Catava. "We are friends."

"I mean it, Catava. No lion—not even Sayid, especially not Sayid—can know."

"Malika, dear, you are my friend. You have my word."

"Promise me."

"I promise!"

Regretfully, Malika called for the tiger cub beyond the concealment of the den. As Bohdan's little body broke free of the dense foliage that covered the den's entrance, Catava was shocked at what she saw.

"What is this? What is this?" she asked in exasperation as she examined the tiger cub intently.

Malika cuddled the little one and reminded Catava of her promise. "You must keep your word!"

"Are you insane? This is forbidden; you are going to get us killed! Malika, what are you thinking?"

"No, no, no; no lion has to find out!" insisted Malika.

"This is treachery!" Catava stated as she angrily shook her head in disbelief. She then took a step forward to get a closer look at the bizarre cub. "Look at those green eyes, those big feet—that face and those stripes!"

She was actually enthralled by the beauty of this strange being but the consequences of being associated with such an outsider, let alone including it in the midst of the pride, overwhelmed her and without warning Catava bolted. Malika knew that she must not let Catava get away, so she thrust Bohdan back into the den and launched into a full-out sprint. Catava's youth gave her a substantial lead, but she was soon reminded why Malika was the lead hunter of the pride.

Malika swiftly caught up with Catava and with one giant leap grabbed hold of her hindquarters, which caused both lionesses to tumble violently to the ground. A struggle immediately ensued. The skillful Malika quickly pinned Catava to the ground.

Between gasps for breath, Malika delivered her warning, "Even though—we are friends, I will kill you—if you continue—to struggle."

Catava surrendered to Malika's admonition without another word.

Still breathing with some effort, Malika warned Catava yet again. "Re-remember your promise! I will die—before I let any harm come—to—my cub."

A bewildered Catava responded, "Malika, what—what—are you saying? What you're doing is punishable by death!"

"Then so be it; it's a chance I am willing to take!"

"What is it about that…that strange creature for which you are willing to risk your life?"

Malika released her hold on Catava. "He needs me. He needs us all." Then she turned and regally sauntered back towards her den.

In The Shadows

Chapter III
King's
Quandary

Images of the freakish cub weighed heavily on Catava's mind. Nevertheless, she was able to make it back to the pride in time to eat and gather up scraps for her cubs. King Sayid was not pleased that she had not assisted in the hunt. She was one of the better hunters in the pride and her absence hindered their ability to bring down prey of substantial size. Despite his dissatisfaction with Catava, the King was curious to learn of Malika's status.

Sensing that something was amiss, King Sayid purposefully approached Catava to solicit information about the condition of his grieving queen.

"So, how is she?" King Sayid inquired.

Catava, visibly disturbed by the question, ignored the King while pondering the fate of Malika and her foreign cub.

Sayid took her response to imply that Malika's condition had not improved; somewhat disheartened, he slowly walked away.

As Catava made her way back to her den, she realized that she was in a delicate situation. She was torn between her loyalty to the king and her friend's deadly secret. She couldn't help but dwell on the consequences that were sure to come and wondered why the elder lioness was so intent on committing such treachery.

Thunder clapped and lightning slashed across the sky, confirming that a major storm was imminent. Thick rain clouds darkened the mid-afternoon sky as Catava lay restlessly in her den with her cubs. Sleep eluded her because of the internal struggle concerning Malika and Sayid. Suddenly, her ears perked and a wide smile covered her face. She recognized the familiar scent of Sayid.

Though she was uncomfortable being second to Malika, Catava was very proud to be the King's concubine. The shrubbery at the entrance of the den ruffled gently as Sayid entered.

"Daddy, daddy," Faraji and Kisa called.

"Hello, my little ones. Come give your dad a hug, then go outside to play. I need some time with your mother," Sayid commanded, as he gave Catava a seductive smile.

The cubs obliged and left the den to play before the rain began to fall. The young lioness enthusiastically offered herself to Sayid, and when he was done, he abruptly pulled away.

"I need to check on Malika. She should be back with the pride by now."

Catava nuzzled Sayid's massive mane and spoke respectfully, so as not to incur his wrath. "Sire, I was just with Malika yesterday and she is fine. There is no need for you to rush off to her. I will check on her again before tonight's hunt."

"Catava, Malika is still my queen and the pride is in desperate need of her participation. After all, I haven't seen her in several Eyes now."

Sayid stretched his shoulders and hindquarters before attempting to leave the den. However, Catava blocked his way and pled, "Sayid, trust me, she's fine." Coaxingly, she added, "Come here and allow me to groom your mane."

"Catava, you do this every time I am unable to stay at length. I have business to attend and right now, that business is Malika!"

Sayid brushed past Catava and headed toward the mouth of the den.

Blind with rage, her envy succumbed to reason and Catava yelled, "Rush then! Rush to your precious Malika and realize just what a traitor she is!"

At this, Sayid stood motionless for what seemed like several minutes but were only mere seconds. He turned to face Malika's accuser.

"Traitor?" he asked, disconcertedly. "What do you mean, traitor?"

Immediately regret overwhelmed Catava. She was visibly shaken but desperate to keep Sayid's favor.

"There is a feline cub that has the stripes of a zebra; Malika nurtures this cub. That is why she has not joined the hunt. That is why she has not come to you, my king."

"You do not speak the truth. How absurd, a feline cub with zebra stripes?"

"Yes, Sayid. I couldn't believe my eyes but what I say is true. She called it her cub."

"And this zebra cub lives with Malika?"

"Mm hmm."

"And she is seeing to it as her own?"

"Yes. I am sorry. Please don't let Malika know I told you," beseeched Catava. "I promised her."

"Save your apology for another Eye and your promises for a more worthy lioness. I must see to this at once!" boomed King Sayid.

He angrily hastened to Malika's den as Catava dragged herself to the darkest corner of her own and began to weep.

King Sayid crossed the plain in virtually no time, thanks to his swift stride. He slowed down a few meters from the opening of Malika's dwelling, not only to compose himself, but to catch his breath as well. He wanted to appear regal and in control instead of confused and bewildered.

Sayid took slow, deliberate steps as he entered Malika's den unannounced.

Shocked by the sight of a pariah in the presence of his queen, Sayid called out in a commanding voice, "Malika, what is this treason?"

Startled, Malika instinctively protected the cub. Upon realizing the king's intrusiveness, she could only mutter "sire" in a show of respect.

"I should kill you both for this treachery, or better yet, if you don't kill it immediately, I'll kill the pariah myself and you'll be furthermore banished from our pride."

"Sayid, he's just a cub," pleaded Malika, still shielding Bohdan from the king.

"He is not a lion! Just look at that thing. It's an abomination," Sayid said contemptuously, tossing his head for dramatic effect.

"I have looked at him and he is the most beautiful creature I have ever seen."

"Beautiful? It has stripes and green eyes. Get rid of it now," he roared.

"I will not," declared Malika defiantly.

"Yes, you will—or die."

Tired of arguing and knowing her place in Sayid's heart, Malika entreated, "I know you love me and I believe you loved our cubs. Allow me this chance to be a mother again, Sayid."

"My queen, I do love you but you know the law; all mongrels must be put to death! He simply must die!"

"I know the law, but you are king!"

"If you keep this atrocity, the pride will be up in paws and there is no telling what kind of chaos will ensue. If it stays, I will not be responsible for its safety or for yours."

Malika replied with venom. "You weren't responsible for the safety of our cubs when they were devoured by the jaws of the river lizards, so what's the difference in you not protecting us now? Where were you then, Sayid? Out hunting? Uh, no! Taking a nap? Hmm, no! Who were you with? Do our cub's siblings live? Or have you allowed more cubs to die?"

Malika's instincts were correct about Sayid being with another lioness but she did not suspect Catava.

Sayid stared at her in disbelief. He was remorseful for the pain he had caused Malika but that sentiment soon turned to anger at her disrespectful tone.

Struggling with his conflicting feelings, Sayid only replied, "I will leave you and your stubbornness to your fate. If you are found out, I will deny knowledge of this betrayal and allow the pride to handle the matter as they deem necessary."

With that said, Sayid stalked off, allowing a temporary reprieve for Malika and Bohdan.

Sayid could not comprehend Malika's behavior and the unusual creature she was so determined to protect. As he returned to the gathering grounds, he was met by five of the ten sentinels of the pride. The sentinels consisted of senior female lionesses and elder males who were wise but too old to mate or rule. The pride also contained guardians and sizzies. Guardians were male lions that didn't have the bloodline of the king; therefore, they were unable to rule. Their only objective was to be loyal to the king by protecting him and members of the pride against enemies.

A chosen few were allowed to mate but only with lionesses approved by the king, for the sole purpose of increasing the pride's population. Sizzies were female lions that were often offspring of the guardians. Their role in the pride was to mate, hunt and provide protection when necessary.

"Sire, we have utterances that the integrity of the pride may be threatened!" announced the first sentinel.

"Where is this threat and why haven't I been notified?"

"We don't know, sire. At this point, the intelligence is unconfirmed," reported another sentinel.

"So, do we even know the source of this rumor and what type of threat is involved?" the king questioned.

"No, sire, but if the rumors are true, the existence of the pride could be in peril, even more so for all those involved," declared Omar, who was the longest tenured sentinel in the pride.

"What are you implying, Omar?" King Sayid demanded.

"Nothing, sire. I was just iterating the severity of the situation."

"Until we can determine the type of threat, I will determine the severity—is that understood?" King Sayid retorted.

"Yes, sire."

"You are dismissed!"

Sayid then retreated to his mound to contemplate his quandary. He was stunned to know that some of the sentinels might already have specific knowledge of Malika's treachery. He endured a sleepless day as he pondered what course of action he should follow with his queen.

When morning dawned, Sayid made a brief, clandestine visit to Malika's lair again.

He stopped just short of the opening of the den and called for her.

When she warily appeared, Sayid informed her, "You are safe for now my dear, but either kill that atrocity or keep it hidden until you hear more from me." Before Malika could reply, he was gone.

The seniors remained silent about how the rumor of this particular threat had begun but nevertheless, they were determined to get to the bottom of the mystery. The senior sentinels were well aware of the penalties that would be incurred if they were caught in the presence of the queen, let alone questioning her. No male was allowed to be in her vicinity unless ordered by the king. Violators were either banished or killed—without exception.

Consequently, the sentinels dispatched a couple of underlings to interrogate Catava. It was no secret that Catava and Malika were close associates and that Catava was known as a chatterbox. The subordinates threatened to force her to watch as they kill both of her cubs, if she didn't confess all she knew about Malika and the alleged infiltrator.

Catava calmly and carefully answered all of their questions, making sure to save herself and her cubs, but not to overtly implicate Malika.

"I remember Malika acting very strange and nervous the last time I saw her. I never saw a striped thing. I guess she could have been hiding something. Do you really think she would risk destroying the pride?"

The two sentinels did not answer her, but returned to report what Catava had told them. The elder of the two noticed something peculiar about Catava's remarks. When they returned to their waiting colleagues, he went straight to Omar.

"Senior Omar, I believe Catava has seen the intruder. We never mentioned stripes, yet this is how she describes the threat. Shall we take the other sentinels and do away with Malika?"

"No, not yet," cautioned Omar. "We still have no proof."

Now fearful that the seniors would make good on their threat against her life and her cubs, Catava surreptitiously ran off to inform the king of her exchange with them.

"Oh, Sayid, I fear I have made a mess. The sentinels came to see me and I may have mentioned the striped one. They made me so nervous. I said I didn't see it and Malika was acting strange-"

"Silence!" yelled the king, angrily. "You've never been one to hold your tongue." He sighed deeply and then shouted at Catava, "Leave me!"

Chapter IV

Dissension

Growing more and more uneasy with his new found ammunition, Omar paced incessantly. The rumors were now rampant, yet unconfirmed. He set up a meeting with the rest of the sentinels and convinced them to go against the king's rule that the queen was free from harassment. He encouraged them to covertly dispatch a spy to her den and report back any findings of a striped cub.

The spy was shocked and disgusted when he spotted Malika caring for an outsider.

Having seen enough and fearful that he would be discovered, the spy promptly returned to the sentinels to tell them of what he had observed at Malika's den.

Fortunately, King Sayid had already received word that Bohdan had been spotted. Armed with this new information in addition to Catava's near confession, he called an assembly to reveal the striped one and cease all rumors. Malika and Bohdan were present during the king's unveiling and were guarded by Zihad, one of the king's most faithful guardians. The pride was astonished to see a foreign cub in the presence of their queen and taken aback by the decision of both the king and queen to allow the cub to live. They vociferously expressed their disdain for the young intruder with most of their anger being directed at the king.

"This is preposterous!" shouted one lion.

"Treason!" shouted another.

One lioness even speculated that Malika had gone outside of her bond with Sayid and mated with a "Monster."

Finally, after a few minutes of raucous contention, Omar's anger erupted. "This striped one is an abomination, your honor. His mere existence here threatens ours and defies the most sacred oath. Therefore, his demise must not be evaded!"

The fuming pride roared with agreement.

Omar then requested silence, cleared his throat and recited from memory, "Ahem, hmm. The king shall—

without hesitation or regret—immediately destroy any living being, lions included, that compromises the pride and the integrity of the bloodline!"

King Sayid responded sardonically. "Thank you Omar, I thought your memory was beginning to fail you but it seems as though you have proven me wrong." Without waiting for a reply, Sayid continued, "I am the king, and if I deem it necessary, under extenuating circumstances, the creature in question shall be given a reprieve."

This declaration brought forth another round of furious roars from the crowd.

"That's deplorable! I never thought I'd see the day-"

"It's treachery! That's not part of the oath!"

"He's changing the rules! Can he do that?"

Then, a new chant rose amongst the sentinels: "Kill the cub!"

"I'll kill him if the king doesn't want to!" offered a younger senior eagerly.

"Mutiny! Mutiny!" shouted another.

King Sayid was in a precarious predicament. He couldn't have agreed more with the judgment of the pride but he couldn't bear to cause Malika any more pain. King Sayid roared angrily to regain order and civility. "I am still king! And my word is what you will follow. Until I decide otherwise, the striped one is to be regarded as a guest and is not to be harmed in any way. If any of you defy my demands, all who are involved will be killed without delay."

Tears of admiration crept down Malika's face. She was defiantly regal as she sauntered proudly to take her place by her king. While addressing the angry pride, King Sayid specifically made eye contact with the seniors. He wanted to convey, by his expression, that his threat was serious and that any efforts to defy his orders without implicating themselves would be perilous. Also, by referring to 'the striped one' as a guest, Sayid hoped to convince some, that his decision was not as reprehensible as they believed.

The king's clever use of words appeared to fall on deaf ears. The pride was outraged that he had chosen not to honor the sacred oath that all prides follow and had been in existence for eons. Despite the king's threat, there was talk among the seniors of overthrowing him and killing Bohdan as well, although this task was easier said than done. Even if they were successful in killing King Sayid, they would also have to kill Malika, in addition to the king's loyal guardians. Such an act would most certainly seal the fate of the pride. As a result, the idea of dethroning the king was set aside —for now.

Chapter V

Banished

A couple of days passed and Sayid was still very much disturbed about the near rebellion at the assembly. He understood that if he did not take decisive action soon, the damage to his kingship would be irreversible. He decided to visit Malika to ensure she was protected and to make another passionate plea for her to dispose of the strange cub for the sake of the pride.

As Sayid entered Malika's den, he noticed that the little nuisance was playful and full of energy. Caught off-guard by the king's visit, Malika inadvertently placed Bohdan in grave danger. She only had time to gasp upon realizing that her lapse in vigilance had allowed Sayid to stand between her and her cub. Bohdan was totally oblivious to the severity of his predicament and naively tried to nuzzle against Sayid but was immediately rejected by a firm nudge and a menacing growl. Unfazed, Bohdan returned the snarl and then moved away to continue frolicking.

For a brief moment, Sayid thought of killing the cub with one swipe of his paw, but his love for Malika was just enough to give him pause. Instead, the king stared at the undesirable guest in bewilderment, not only because of his captivating appearance, but for the confounding display of courage he had never witnessed in a lion cub. This indecision by Sayid was just enough to allow Malika to recover from her breach. She embraced the tiger cub with a motherly hug that immediately got the king's attention. Convinced that nothing short of a fight to the death would cause Malika to ever give up her young oddity, Sayid left the den without a word being spoken.

Meanwhile, Omar was still furious about the king's decision and he was not alone. The consensus among the pride was that the striped one had to die, and soon. Omar called a secret meeting with the sole purpose of creating a foolproof plan to dethrone Sayid and kill Bohdan while keeping the pride intact. However, the discussion was abruptly cut short when one of the king's faithful guardians approached.

Later that day, while most of the cubs were mischievously cavorting in the sun, Bohdan stared out of the den with a small twinge of desire. He had begun to socialize with other cubs under the watchful eye of Malika but only during dawn and dusk when the temperature was at its lowest. His body still hadn't adapted to the extreme heat in this harsh environment. He was also experiencing a degree of disassociation resulting from the traumatic events that had separated him from his family.

Searching for answers, he asked Malika, "Vhy don't any of the other cubs have stripes like me? Vhy am I so different? Vhy don't the others like me?"

Malika nuzzled the cub and attempted to answer these difficult questions. "Oh, my little magnificent one, you are so full of questions today. I'm sure there are others like you with stripes that are just as fascinating. You wouldn't be different to them. We lions are bred deep in old traditions and not too willing to depart from the ways of those before us. You are just as precious as any other Nomads cub—in some ways, even more so. Don't listen to the others when they call you names. You must remain brave and strong and remember that they are only envious and perhaps a little intimidated because they have never seen anything as beautiful as you."

"Vill I be a lion like King Sayid vone day?"

"No, my precious one, you'll be much more."

With that, Bohdan cuddled closer to his surrogate mother and watched as the other cubs sparred in the hot sun. Soon after, Malika was joined and pressured by the other lionesses to participate in an imminent hunt. While Sayid's admonition at the assembly was comforting, Malika wasn't yet convinced that the atmosphere was safe enough to leave Bohdan alone. After some serious paw-twisting by Catava and mentally assuring herself that Bohdan would be okay, she agreed.

The lionesses and the remaining participating members of the pride moved toward the setting sun as one of the faithful guardians, Zihad and senior Omar were tasked to remain behind to watch over the cubs and patrol the perimeter.

Omar pretended to ignore the cubs as they began to wander and play. Unbeknownst to them, he was very cognizant of all of their whereabouts and even more focused on Malika's den, where little Bohdan lay shielded from the heat.

While wandering with her brother, Kisa—who was Catava's daughter—headed toward Malika's den to coax Bohdan out to play. She and Bohdan were fond of each other, but the relationship between her brother and Bohdan was tense and acrimonious. Faraji adamantly rejected having Bohdan tag along and would leave his sister to go play with the other cubs. Meanwhile, Bohdan remained obedient and refused to leave the den. Malika specifically explained to him that he shouldn't, under any circumstance, vacate the cover of the den while she was not present. If he did, he could be seriously injured or worse.

Despite the stern warning from his surrogate mother, Bohdan found it too overwhelming to resist his curiosity, as well as Kisa, whose coquettish influence was just enough to drive the little cub to cautiously leave the concealment of the den.

When he was spotted by the other cubs, they immediately began to tease him about his exotic appearance.

"Why you got those funny green eyes? They look like emerald demon eyes," one cub taunted.

"Look at those snaky stripes all over his body and face!" exclaimed another.

"Go back to where you came from!" yelled Faraji.

"You should get there quick with those big feet like an *ephalant*," teased another cub.

"Leave him alone, and its *elephant*," chided Kisa.

"Whatever," he replied to Kisa, dismissively. But to Bohdan, he jeered, "You're a demon-eyed snakaphant."

The whole crowd began to chant: "Snakaphant, snakaphant, demon-eyed snakaphant!"

"I am not that much different than you, I'm better!" Bohdan retorted in his thick accent.

"Hey, he even talks funny, vlah, vlah, vlah," yet another cub taunted.

"Leave him alone. Remember what my father said?"

Kisa tried to defend her friend but quickly became a target of taunts.

"What are you, his cub friend?"

"We can put stripes on you and you'll be twins!" The cubs roared with laughter and chants of "snakaphant" could still be heard. Even though Faraji abhorred Kisa's bond with the stranger, he valiantly stepped in to defend his little sister.

"All right, all right. Lay off my sister. C'mon, Jelani, I don't want to catch stripes" he called to his best friend.

The other cubs eventually lost interest and agreed. "I don't want to catch stripes either," then trotted off after Faraji and Jelani.

Omar and Zihad had been watching the cubs' interaction with Bohdan from afar. Outraged to see the foreign cub and Kisa's camaraderie, Omar stalked away in disgust.

Although Zihad appeared undisturbed by the strange sight of a foreign cub among the lion adolescents, he was unable to keep his eyes off of him. He was especially drawn in wonderment to the strange zebra-like stripes and his abnormally large paws.

Omar, still livid at the king's decision to allow a foreign cub to remain in the midst of the pride, waited until he was some distance from the camp before fully conveying his anger in the form of a tantrum.

"*HZZZZZZZZZ, HZZZZZZZZZZ!*"

He was so engrossed in his fury that all of his senses were momentarily numb, even his normally impeccable hearing. Omar didn't initially register the loud hissing directed toward him and he all but stepped on one of the few inhabitants of the region that demanded more respect than King Sayid himself. The giant king cobra, Ophious, was twenty feet in length and possessed venom so potent that it could kill a grown elephant in three hours.

He hissed a warning once more, *"HZZZZZZZZ!"*

Before Omar could react, the big cobra rose with his hood expanded and the upright portion of his body swayed from one side to the other in a circular motion. Now, with the cobra's fangs only inches away from his face, Omar froze, realizing that he was mere seconds away from the kiss of death. Ophious quickly took advantage of the lion's hesitation and wrapped part of his elongated body around Omar's back and anchored himself to one of the elder lion's hindquarters.

The old lion attempted to resist falling under the spell of the rhythmic dance of the serpent but Ophious's hypnotic eyes were inescapable at this distance.

The deadly serpent hissed his final warning. "I am very much liking death for your insolence. Speak your last."

Ophious then constricted so that Omar could feel the extent of his strength. Although Omar was old and much slower than he had been in his prime, he remained astute enough to realize he had only one chance to save his life.

The lion struggled to reply under the immense pressure of Ophious's coils. Miraculously, he was able to break eye contact with the serpent long enough to speak coherently.

"P-p-pardon my audaciousness, Your Majesty. If you spare your serpent's kiss, as payment for my indignity, perhaps I can offer a tastier resolution."

Attention gained, Ophious began to release his grip. Omar gasped for air, while elaborating on his scheme to lead the cobra back to Malika's den and have him devour the tiger cub before the rest of the pride returned. Omar must make it appear that the cobra had come between him and Bohdan, which would leave him helpless.

Believing he had a solid alibi, Omar led Ophious back to Malika's den. He smiled to himself as he envisioned the accolades he would receive from the pride once the demon zebra cub met his demise.

Just before reaching the thick brush that concealed Malika's den, the senior lion advised Ophious to await his command.

The king cobra anticipated the taste of the cub and began to salivate.

Impatiently, he snapped at Omar. "No commands should you be giving me."

Extremely wary and not wanting to fall victim to the quick tempered cobra's deadly venom, Omar nervously persuaded Ophious to give him a moment to set the trap. Meanwhile, Faraji and Jelani had gone to the far end of the camping ground to spar with some of the older cubs. Unsupervised, the other cubs continued to tease Bohdan as he and Kisa headed back to Malika's den together.

"Hey, Stripy, are you half zebra? Yeah, let's hear you squeal like a zebra."

However, the taunts instantly halted at Omar's approach. He admonished the lion cubs for associating with such an abominable creature and demanded that they return to their respective dens at once.

The cubs scattered promptly without a word. Just then, guardian Zihad approached Omar and questioned his actions. "Senior, the king's orders were to..." Omar interrupted Zihad mid-sentence. "YOUR ORDERS are to patrol the perimeter and as your elder, I demand you do so at once!"

Zihad contemplated challenging Omar's demands but decided otherwise and pretended to leave on patrol. He sensed that the senior was behaving strangely so he concealed himself in the tall grass to see what Omar would do next. Believing that the guardian had left, Omar gave Ophious the signal to proceed, unaware that Kisa had followed Bohdan into Malika's den.

The tall grass momentarily prevented Zihad from getting a clear view of the senior's devious scheme. It also prevented the cobra from obtaining a clear visual of Malika's den until he lengthened his body upward to confirm his path.

Once Zihad saw the hood of the cobra rising above the grass line and heading toward the location of the cubs, he attacked without a second thought, while emitting a roar that could be heard from miles away. Omar tried to confront the guardian but was easily plowed over by the younger, stronger lion.

Before Ophious could gain entry, Zihad sank his fangs and claws deep into the giant cobra's back and attempted to pull him away from the den's opening. Zihad was able to pull Ophious just far back enough to allow room for the cubs to escape. To his surprise and dismay, Bohdan refused to flee.

Instead, Bohdan courageously shielded Kisa from the venom-dripping fangs of the cobra. He crouched down in a defensive posture, ready to combat the cobra to the death if necessary.

Brandishing his underdeveloped incisors, Bohdan let out what he believed to be a mighty roar but in actuality, it was simply a meek "rowr."

While Zihad struggled to keep his grip on the twisting cobra, he was attacked from the rear by Omar. The older lion seized a mouthful of Zihad's mane in an attempt to force the guardian into releasing his grip on the cobra. As Zihad tried to fight off Omar and control his grip on Ophious, he briefly glimpsed Bohdan eye to eye.

For a split second, he was amazed by the cub's bravery, before gasping his last command.

"GET OUT!"

At that moment, Ophious whipped his head back and sank his three-inch fangs deep into the guardian's side, pumping lethal amounts of venom through the lion's body.

Immediately weakened by the deadly toxin, Zihad had little fight left and relinquished his hold on the cobra. Omar then released Zihad, just as the pride returned in a stampede, responding to Zihad's initial roar of distress. Ophious, who was severely injured, gave up on his meal and slithered slowly into the underbrush, just before the first members of the pride arrived.

The first to survey the scene were Malika and Catava, who were greeted by loud roaring and exaggerated sobbing from Omar as he stood over the motionless guardian. Malika initially failed to acknowledge the deceased guardian and Omar's theatrics. Her only concern was whether or not Bohdan was safe. She immediately called out to Bohdan which prompted both him and Kisa to come into view. Malika was relieved that her young one was safe, but Catava, although relieved as well, was not so pleased to see Kisa and Bohdan together.

Now that he had an audience, Omar began to yell, "THE DEMON ZEBRA CUB KILLED HIM! THE DEMON STRIPED ONE IS A KILLER AND A FRIEND OF THE DEATH SERPENTS."

Omar pointed his forepaw at Malika's den, where Bohdan and Kisa stood. The rest of the pride began to chime in as well with their false accusations and outrageous claims of Bohdan's evil nature.

King Sayid's approach brought immediate silence. The lions parted to allow him access to the site and the fallen guardian. As the gruesome tragedy that had occurred only moments before came into view, the king slowed his pace; his favorite guardian now lay dead in his path.

Omar intercepted Sayid before he could reach Zihad's remains. He motioned to Bohdan and Malika, demanding that they both be killed. The pride, ignited by his impassioned rhetoric, voiced their approval of his plan.

Sayid briefly contemplated the gravity of the situation. He loved Malika and didn't want to kill her but she loved the very creature that had caused so much upheaval.

With a loud roar, Sayid once more brought the pride to silence and demanded that Malika dispatch the cub immediately or die. Shouts of encouragement came from the crowd, who preferred to see the traitor and her undesirable cub executed.

Malika was livid at Sayid's condemnation and responded poignantly "Never!"

The pride growled angrily at Malika's blatant insubordination and increasingly became more aggressive with insults and paw swipes in her direction to show their disdain.

Sayid immediately ordered the remaining guardians to keep the angry lions at bay. Next, he walked midway down the path previously created for him and pondered the possibility of Malika's execution. His love for Malika was too strong to allow the pride to administer their brutal form of capital punishment. Instead, Sayid determined that if Malika were to be exiled from the pride, neither she nor the cub would survive for long.

He then turned to face his queen. With some difficulty, Sayid announced somberly, "Malika, you and your beloved pariah are forever more banished to Mortis Bode and beyond. Should either one of you be seen by Nomads again, you will be hunted and killed."

Kisa gasped in disbelief as her father exiled her close friend. She immediately turned to her mother to explain what really happened.

"Mama, Bohdan didn't have anything to do with guardian Zihad's death! It was-"

"Hush, Kisa," Catava admonished in a loud whisper, hoping no one else had heard her daughter.

"Go straight home." Catava ordered.

But another cub did hear Kisa and came to her defense, telling his mother, "Kisa's right, the snakaphant didn't-" However, he too was shushed by his mother.

Head held high, Sayid returned silently to his mound. Malika was stunned at Sayid's irrational decision and after taking a moment to collect her thoughts, stood erect and happened to catch the eye of Catava. For a second or two, Malika believed that she would at least find some degree of comfort or neutrality in the eyes of her closest friend but to her dismay, Catava turned her head in disgust. Malika showed no emotion in response to Catava's snub as she and Bohdan turned away and began their walk towards Mortis Bode.

Chapter VI
Chokka's Abode

Mortis Bode was a perilous, impermeable forest. It was infested with ferocious animals, insects, venomous reptiles, toxic plants and numerous obscure bottomless pits that reeked of death from the many unsuspecting lives randomly claimed. The forest was so dangerous that the Nomads did not dare to venture past its outer edges. They were more accustomed to open plains where they could observe their prey more clearly.

Moreover, the large trees and vast number of bottomless pits would impede their efforts to work effectively as a team to bring down larger prey. Prey that were unfamiliar with this region and lucky enough to escape the lions, naturally sought solace in the forest, a decision that often proved to be deadlier than several prides of lions.

Malika and Bohdan remained silent on their walk to
Mortis Bode. She was pained that King Sayid would
succumb to such outrageous accusations and antiquated
prejudices. Although she was curious to know what had
caused the tragic demise of a dear friend, it was
inconceivable that little Bohdan had any role in the death of
a fully grown lion.

Bohdan also walked with a heavy heart. He was
saddened that he would never see Kisa again. In spite of the
pride's abhorrence of his very existence, she was the only
one who had befriended him.

The journey to Mortis Bode was not a long one. Soon,
Malika and Bohdan found themselves facing the thick
foliage of the forest. Malika paused and took a deep breath
before penetrating the outer edge of the wood line. She
tried to remain calm and brave for Bohdan, but she was
extremely nervous and rightfully so. According to the
legend, no lion had ever entered Mortis Bode and returned
alive.

Malika also sensed they were being followed. With
every upward glance, she noticed that the dark, clustered
canopy of tree limbs and vegetation held a myriad of
openings that allowed flickers of moonlight and starlight to

enter. Malika was convinced that two of the flickers were a pair of yellow eyes, seeming to anticipate their every move.

Bohdan, on the other hand, was unaware of the legend surrounding the forest. Instead, he was simply curious about his new surroundings. He also appeared to be unfazed by the unfamiliar sounds and the incessant stench of death inundating the forest.

Malika's observation was true. Mortis Bode had many eyes and two in particular had indeed noticed the arrival of the lioness and the strange, striped cub.

The black jaguar named Chokka was known as the assassin of the night and was the most dangerous predator of the forest. He liked to lurk high in the trees, usually coming down only to hunt and to protect his territory. Though smaller in stature compared to a fully grown tiger or lion, Chokka was a formidable, compact and well-muscled opponent that could bring down prey three times his size.

In addition, as a jaguar, Chokka was extremely stealthy—one of his most feared attributes. His victims were rarely aware of his presence until it was too late. His dark fur blended well against the night, allowing the jaguar to skulk within inches of his prey before unleashing a deadly assault.

Back within the Nomads' territory, Sayid reflected upon his decision to exile Malika. The pride was calling for blood, so he had been forced to act. Nonetheless, Sayid felt that there was more to Zihad's death than Omar led him to believe.

The more he thought about Omar's story, the more suspicious he became. Sayid called Omar to his side.

"I need you to go after Malika."

"Into Mortis Bode, sire?" Omar was rather puzzled by the request.

"You must find her. Do not return without her."

"Yes, sire," Omar said, obediently.

Omar started to walk in the direction of Mortis Bode. He was staggered that the king had chosen him to enter the forbidden forest instead of an expendable guardian. Just then, he heard the king call his name. Hoping for a reprieve from this daunting task, he expectantly turned to Sayid.

"Yes, sire?"

"Dispose of the striped one."

"Happily, sire!"

Omar temporarily suppressed his fears and within hours, he had amazingly caught up with Malika and Bohdan, deep in the forest.

Malika was alarmed by Omar's presence. She immediately pushed Bohdan to her rear, shielding him from any potential assault by the pernicious senior.

"Queen Malika, your presence is requested back with the pride."

"I am no longer your queen, liar!" Malika responded.

"I speak the truth. The king would like nothing more than for you to return to his side." Omar stressed.

Overjoyed, Malika naively exclaimed, "C'mon, Bohdan, it's time to go home."

"Oh, no, not so fast," Omar snidely remarked. He looked around nervously at his unfamiliar surroundings. He clarified, "Your presence—not his. King Sayid commands that you rid us of this awful creature and return to him at once."

"Omar, my cub needs me. I just can't leave him."

"The Nomads need your skills and the king wants your companionship."

"I will not return without Bohdan," insisted Malika.

"I implore you; the king demands your return and the execution of this abomination."

"I won't do it."

"If you refuse, I will take matters into my own claws."

"Do what you must."

"Your wish…" Omar spitefully roared as he launched a forceful assault upon Malika.

Bohdan attempted to defend his surrogate mother but was quickly shoved aside as Malika attempted to fight off the larger male lion. Unusually cognizant of his surroundings, Bohdan instinctively climbed up the nearest tree for safety. Little did he know, he was not alone.

Omar continued his assault on Malika. He charged wildly but Malika managed to sidestep his advance causing the senior to miss his target. Snarling with frustration, Omar attacked again. This time he landed a solid blow that stunned Malika momentarily; however, she recovered quickly and landed several strikes of her own, keeping Omar at bay for the moment.

Having gotten his second wind, the larger male began to drive Malika backwards with a series of strikes that put her on the defensive. Malika tried to stand her ground but to avoid being pummeled by Omar's assault, she retreated briefly to regroup. Unfortunately, during her retreat, Malika lost her footing and plummeted to her death into one of the forest's many bottomless pits.

Bloodied and exhausted, the battered senior turned his attention to Bohdan, who remained in a large tree. Though unaccustomed to climbing trees, Omar was determined to kill Bohdan once and for all. As the big male struggled to climb the tree, Bohdan retreated higher, but eventually found himself at the end of a relatively short limb.

Omar was so intent on killing the tiger cub that he was unaware of how high he had climbed. The senior lion continued to inch closer to Bohdan, taunting the cub who was now only a couple of yards away.

With no means of escape, Bohdan's tiger instincts took over. He bluffed the determined senior with a powerful little growl and a mock charge, while hissing and brandishing his juvenile canines. Omar was momentarily stunned by this act of aggression and abruptly halted his ascent. Before the big lion could gather his bearings and continue his assault, he was stupefied by another roar twenty times more thunderous than Bohdan's, which temporarily made him lose his grip on the tree.

This time, the roar had originated from Chokka, the fearless black jaguar. He had watched the entire event unfold and having no tolerance for intruders, stealthily crawled down from his perch, adjacent to Bohdan. Now, he stood between the big lion and the bizarre little cub.

"Getchur kicks terrorizing females and cubs, Brownie?" Chokka smirked.

Still struggling to regain his hold, Omar recovered in time to shoot back, "You dare to interfere with the king's business, you reject?"

Chokka looked down at the ground below to his left, and then brought his gaze back to the lion's eyes, speaking deliberately. "Your dastardly leader has no authority here and neither do you, brown back."

Infuriated by the jaguar's disrespect, Omar gathered his footing and pompously stated, "For your vile indignity, I will take the utmost pleasure in killing you, as well as the abomination."

Instantaneously Omar attempted to strike Chokka, but the jaguar was a fierce and adept fighter in the trees. Anticipating Omar's advance, he evaded the lion's assault and countered with lightning speed striking the lion near the temporal area with a traumatic blow that caused the precariously balanced foe to lose his grip and fall.

Omar crashed through limb after limb eventually hitting the ground with a loud thud.

Now relieved of the imminent threat of the senior, Bohdan's focus returned to Malika as he gingerly made his way down the tree to peer into the gaping hole in which Malika had fallen.

A pitiful "rowr" escaped him as he lay down by the edge as if expecting her to climb out soon.

Chokka had quietly followed the cub down the tree and in an unsympathetic tone asked, "So, what's your story, Stripy?"

Unsure of Chokka's intentions, Bohdan took a moment
to respond. He was in awe of Chokka's muscular build and
silky black coat, but his ominous, emotionless stare was
perplexing. Bohdan reflected back to moments shared with
Malika when she encouraged him to remain brave and
strong. He then stood erect and corrected the jaguar.

"My name is Bohdan!"

Chokka was impressed by Bohdan's courage and chuckled softly to himself. He took a closer look at the tiger and was amazed by the array of stripes on his coat as well as his unusually large paws. He was equally puzzled by the young cub's peculiar language.

"Hmm," he replied, then looked in the direction of Malika's tragic fall. "Sorry about your loss." The jaguar paused for a moment before returning his focus back to the little tiger. Noticing his emerald green eyes, Chokka continued, "I've roamed Mortis for many years, seen many different kinds of felids, but you, little Bohdan, are the strangest of them all!"

Bohdan responded with a hiss to show that he was becoming uneasy with the jaguars presence and began to cautiously back away.

"Relax, Courage, I'm not gonna hurt ya," Chokka assured, while examining Bohdan with his deep yellow eyes as if he were a brilliant work of art. After reflecting on the recent sequence of events and putting it all in perspective, Chokka opined, "I probably should have let the big brownie have his way with ya. You'll never survive here alone."

Bohdan relaxed his stance slightly and replied boldly,

"I can survive."

Chokka gave Bohdan his ominous blank gaze and a sarcastic smirk. Finally, he said, "Let's get a couple of things straight. If you were a brownie, I would have killed ya myself, understood?" Bohdan lowered his head feeling dejected. "But since you're not, you're safe for now, although I'm a bit curious to know why those brownies were fightin' over ya."

Bohdan didn't answer; he just looked longingly back into the dreadful abyss.

"Aww, that's not important right now. What's important is what to do with ya!" Chokka paced as he pondered this dilemma, then turned to Bohdan and said, "Ya got a choice; stay here and die, or learn to survive."

Bohdan stiffened, then remarked, "I vant to go home!"

Chokka grunted. "And just where is home, Courage?"

Bohdan lowered his head a little as he softly stated, "I don't know."

Chokka was confused for the first time in his adult life. He was unable to comprehend the fascination and admiration he had with this strange-looking feline. Usually known for his unmerciful ferociousness, Chokka was uncharacteristically torn between compassion and heartlessness. For now, compassion was victorious. With a deep sigh, Chokka grumbled reluctantly, "Follow!"

He began to walk away but paused for a moment and gave an unsympathetic warning, "If ya ever cross me, I will kill ya. Ya understand?"

Bohdan replied, "Yes, uh, mmm?"

Chokka quickly answered, "The name's Chokka!"

Back at the Nomads' pride, day to day activities were slowly returning to normal, with the exception of Sayid, who was lying on his mound, still worrying about the status of Malika. It had been three days since he sent the senior to bring back his queen. He was considering sending a couple of guardians to search for signs but before he could complete that thought, he was joined by an unusual guest.

Saabir, a lappet-faced vulture with a wingspan of over ten feet, a razor-sharp beak and massive powerful talons that could rip through flesh with ease, appeared before him. Over the years, Saabir had become King Sayid's eyes and ears from above.

Often, when food was scarce, the lions looked to circling vultures in the sky to lead them to freshly killed prey or carrion. For that convenience, the lions often left the remaining scraps for the vultures while providing protection from others who considered the vultures as prey or competition.

"Goood eeveenniiing, Kiiinng," Saabir greeted in his slow, creaky drawl.

"Saabir," Sayid responded.

He preferred to keep his conversations brief when talking to the vultures because they spoke so slowly and emphatically and Sayid was rather impatient.

"Iiii haaavve neewws," the vulture continued. "A llaargge mmaallee feeelinne caarrcaassss hhaasss beeeeen sseeenn on ttheee edgge oof Mmorrrtisss Boode wiith Nooommaadd esseenncce."

Although Sayid was sympathetic to the demise of senior Omar, he was still hopeful and began to inquire about Malika and Bohdan. "Have you any other news? Perhaps of a lioness accompanied by a striped cub in or around the same vicinity?"

Saabir responded, "Nooo sssiiirrree. Onnlly ooffff the llaargge feeelinne."

The king stared off toward Mortis Bode as he pondered his options. He contemplated again about sending another search for Malika but eventually conceded that such an attempt would be useless.

Finally, Sayid stood up and began to walk away. As he did so, the vulture took flight, saying, "Weee wwillll wwaatchh and lisstennn foorr the llliionnessss and the sstrriippdd ccubbbb, sssiiirrree" as he flew over head.

Chapter VII
Roar!

Under the tutelage of Chokka, Bohdan had amazingly survived the perils of Mortis Bode. Chokka had protected the young tiger from harm since their initial encounter and was astounded that he had survived this long. Usually, cubs of the felidae family are weaned from eight to seven months and then introduced to fresh meat. Only under extreme circumstances would they be weaned earlier, even then, they would rarely survive.

By mimicking Chokka's every move, Bohdan had not only survived but had thrived and grown into a healthy, ferocious killer unlike anything Chokka had ever witnessed in a young cub. At the outset, Chokka grappled with the thought of taking the strange cub under his guidance. Just like tigers, jaguars ordinarily followed solitary lives and this was especially true for Chokka, who hadn't seen a member of his own kind in years. Although this was the first time he had come across a tiger or even knew that such a feline existed, Chokka's deep intuition was that he and his newfound protégé had a lot in common.

Tigers and jaguars are indeed similar in many ways. Stealth is one key characteristic shared by both and is essential for survival.

Chokka's entire existence was based on stealth, so much so that he rarely communicated orally. Through various combinations of eye contact and subtle head movements, Chokka taught Bohdan how to communicate and understand an array of commands and emotions without the faintest utterance.

One of the most noticeable features that tigers and jaguars share is their robust skull structure, enabling the jaw to clamp down in an extremely powerful bite. Most felines kill their prey by biting through the throat of their victims, causing some degree of suffering and a relatively slow demise. Chokka employed a more brutal but merciful method of killing. His jaws were so powerful that he was able to bite through the temporal bones of most his victim's skull, piercing the brain to cause instant death.

Bohdan continued to perfect this method, along with many more invaluable lessons during his tenure with Chokka.

Three rules in particular had been stressed more so than others: dwelling in the trees, avoiding all serpents and only killing to survive, unless provoked. The last rule was one yet to be mastered by Chokka himself. One of the toughest tasks that Bohdan had to learn before making his first solo kill of substantial significance was patience. Chokka made it look easy. He was the master of ambushes and opportunistic hunting, which often required an extraordinary amount of perseverance.

Initially, Bohdan struggled with this concept; he didn't understand why it was necessary to sit in one spot for what seemed like an eternity waiting for potential prey to come along. He preferred the thrill of the chase which up to this point had only yielded an empty belly when hunting larger, agile prey. After several missed meals, young Bohdan quickly realized he had to try a new approach.

One day before dusk, Chokka set up an ambush near a small water hole. He positioned Bohdan on one side and himself on the other amid the thick foliage. He knew it would be at least a couple of hours before any potential prey would seek this particular water spot. The trap was specifically designed to evaluate young Bohdan's concentration in a hostile environment. Unbeknownst to the young tiger, Chokka had intentionally placed him in a location that was teaming with annoying, biting insects. Chokka was astonished at the youngster's resilience.

Bohdan was extremely focused and seemed to all but ignore the flurry of irritants, but after a few hours passed, his patience was under serious duress. In search of some type of reprieve, Bohdan glanced over at his mentor. To his dismay, the conspicuous plea for mercy was ignored.

Shortly thereafter, a young capybara timidly approached the water hole from a nearby clearing. Capybaras are the largest living rodents, resembling huge, tailless rats and can weigh up to two hundred pounds. The rodent instinctively paused to survey the surrounding area for any signs of danger.

Refocused, Bohdan ever so slightly looked to Chokka, seeking the strategy of attack like a pitcher on the mound looking to the hind-catcher for the right pitch. With a subtle movement of his head, Chokka gave the command to remain still. Although wary, the capybara lowered his head and began to sip nervously while still maintaining his vigilance. Bohdan, on the other hand, was on the precipice of losing his mind. He hadn't had fresh meat in days, was thoroughly annoyed with the insects and couldn't understand Chokka's reluctance to allow him to attack. Bohdan made another combination of subtle eye and head movements to suggest he was ready to move. But Chokka's stare was steadfast and conveyed one obvious message: "Wait!"

Seconds later, Bohdan gave Chokka another combination of eye and head movements, and then another. Before long, Bohdan had covered every method of attack in his young repertoire, but Chokka's expression remained unchanged. All the while, the capybara continued to quench his thirst.

Just before Bohdan's patience ran dry, the culmination of Chokka's teaching swept over him like a peaceful breeze caressing the plains before the arrival of torrential rains.

With his eyes trained on Chokka and his pupils dilated, Bohdan gave his mentor a menacing stare that conveyed determination, complete focus, and calm referred to only as Nova.

Nova is an extremely focused frame of mind that overcomes most felidae right before they pounce on their prey. It is the unbreakable mental block of any surrounding distractions, accompanied by a dead stare and culminates with an outburst of raw energy directed at hapless prey or enemies.

Confident that Bohdan had discovered his nova, Chokka slowly nodded his head while widening his eyes. Instantly, Bohdan exploded into action. With his guard relaxed, the capybara didn't have much of a chance. It took Bohdan several moments to deliver the crushing bite but at last, his first solo kill of substantial size was history.

Bohdan was now completely sold on Chokka's way of hunting. He was extremely confident in his ability and eager to tackle larger and more dangerous prey. Although proud and astonished by Bohdan's level of progress given his youth, Chokka was not completely convinced that his young protégé was ready to take on more threatening animals. Therefore, he limited Bohdan's prey to less aggressive quarries like capybaras, jackals, and other diminutive creatures.

One event in particular would not only test Bohdan's ability to kill larger prey, but also confirm what Chokka had been reluctant to acknowledge—that his young protégé was ready to survive alone.

Early one misty morning while perched on a branch of a large tree, Bohdan surveyed the forest floor through an ethereal blanket of mist for his next possible meal. He then spotted a pair of huge adult boars nonchalantly making their way through the thick brush. His immaturity and eagerness to bring down larger prey overshadowed his natural inquisitiveness to assess the dangers associated with unfamiliar conquests.

With a combative attitude and seven inch tusks that could slice through Bohdan's hide with ease, these wild boars would be extremely dangerous to even the most skilled hunters and should not be underestimated. In a separate tree nearby, Chokka was also fixated on the approaching boars. He was very familiar with the ferocity of one boar, let alone two adults, and realized that an attack on two boars at once would be too risky, especially for a young tenderfoot.

Meanwhile, lurking nearby under the foliage of the dense forest floor, a large reticulated python searching for his first meal in weeks, went unnoticed. Bohdan was so anxious to make a kill that he was salivating as he stealthily got in position to jump down on one of the unsuspecting wanderers. Normally, before attacking unfamiliar prey,

Bohdan would seek approval from Chokka but this time Bohdan abandoned all communication. He was in his nova! Chokka had been ignored and needed to act rapidly. The only chance to avoid risking serious injury to either of them was for Chokka to roar, in hopes of scaring off the boars. Unfortunately, the denseness of the forest distorted the direction of the loud rumbling. The approaching boars, now filled with terror and unable to determine the direction of the terrifying roar, ran toward the tree where Bohdan was waiting. He was now in position to attack and allowed the first boar to pass underneath the tree without incident.

However, as the second boar attempted to sprint past, Bohdan leaped down on its back and bit through its skull, killing the fleeing beast instantly. Chokka was now eager to join the action, so as not to be outdone by a felid rookie.

He decided to intervene by cutting off the escape route of the first boar. The frantic beast, realizing that his companion was under serious duress, turned around and made a feeble attempt to intimidate the young tiger by charging and clapping his jaws together, which made a loud popping sound in a display of aggression.

Bloodthirsty and un-intimidated by the boar's bluster, Bohdan released his grip on the head of his victim and displayed his own form of intimidation by unveiling a roar so thunderous, it shook the forest floor and briefly paralyzed the charging antagonist in midstride. The boar tumbled violently to the ground, stopping just short of his fallen comrade and slayer. Now even more terrified than before, the boar staggered to his feet and retreated blindly on course to collide with Chokka, who had also been briefly stunned by Bohdan's monstrous bellow.

Chokka attempted an ill-timed leap over the charging boar to avoid his razor-sharp tusks. Unfortunately, one of his hindquarters was impacted and severely gashed by the tusks of the fleeing quarry. The collision from the boar's tusks was so forceful that it caused Chokka to flip tumultuously in the air before making an ungainly landing in the brush.

To add to the situation, the huge python, unaffected by the roar, set his sights on Bohdan, determined that the young tiger would be his next meal. Normally, pythons would avoid such a commotion but his hunger was overwhelming. The big python lay motionless and unnoticed until precisely the right moment before he attacked the unsuspecting tiger with lightning speed. Bohdan instinctively fought back with reckless abandon to remain free of the python's deadly embrace and snaring fangs.

Significantly injured, Chokka could only watch through the thick brush as his protégé fought for his life. The battle between Bohdan and the python seemed to last for hours.

Bohdan's deafening roar of anger echoed throughout the forest as both combatants were utterly determined to annihilate one another. The python appeared to get the better of Bohdan momentarily as he encircled the feline in his powerful coils. Bohdan felt the intense pressure of the python's squeeze and struggled fiercely to escape its clutches.

Miraculously, he was able to claw, bite and muscle his way free of the python's powerful, bone-crushing grip. Having taken a fairly rough lashing, the python abandoned his attack and fled into the thick, vine-like shrubbery. Bohdan was undeterred by his near fatal encounter and followed to finish the battle but the python managed to slither away.

Meanwhile, Chokka labored to climb a nearby tree to recover in his diminished state. He couldn't believe that Bohdan had survived the clutches of the deadly serpent and never before had he heard a roar so powerful. After abandoning his chase of the python, Bohdan noticed the trail of blood leading up to Chokka's tree. Realizing his mentor was severely injured, Bohdan used his powerful jaws to grab the 250-pound boar carcass by the throat and haul it effortlessly up the tree for Chokka to feast. He believed that the large kill would provide enough nutrients to help Chokka recover quickly.

Full of pride and in immense pain, Chokka stubbornly rejected Bohdan's gesture. "I hunt for myself!" he declared via a clenched jaw.

Bohdan ignored Chokka's rebuff, as he attempted to secure the carcass.

After securing the kill, Bohdan stealthily descended the big tree. Once he reached the bottom, a strange but peculiar event occurred; memories of his young past started to return. Not understanding how or why this was happening, Bohdan looked up at Chokka and exclaimed excitedly, "I can remember now, I believe I can remember now!"

After a few moments of recollection, Bohdan's excitement turned to sorrow as he recalled the traumatic death of his parents. Dejected by these thoughts, he slowly laid down at the base of the tree and stared motionlessly into the distance, while bits and pieces of his memory continued to unite to put the puzzle of his past together.

Unmoved, Chokka simply stared down expressionlessly at Bohdan. He was in too much pain to make any sense of the emotions his young protégé was experiencing. Besides, he had his own cogitations to contend with. Particularly, the sequence of events that resulted in his injury as well as the extraordinary display of survival and courage exhibited by the youngster.

At that moment, there was one thing that was apparently clear to both Bohdan and Chokka; the time had come for the young tiger to leave the protection of his mentor forever to establish his own identity.

Bohdan rose to his paws.

"I am going home!" he announced abruptly.

Chokka remained silent, his blank stare unchanged.

Bohdan began to muse aloud. "I-I'm not sure where home is but I remember the air being much colder than here. The ground and trees vere vhite from an icy powder, and mist vould come out of my mouth and nose vith every breath."

Chokka took a moment before speaking. "Seek the ungulates when the Eye is low and the rains return. If you're lucky, ya may be able to convince one to help ya find your way home—that is, if ya don't kill 'em first."

Bohdan was surprised at such a lengthy statement from Chokka, though he remained indifferent. He nodded his head in agreement, and then slowly turned to walk away.

After a couple of steps, he turned back and looked up at Chokka.

"Are you going to be okay?"

Chokka's yellow eyes continued to stare dispassionately at the tiger while remaining silent.

Bohdan then stood erect and said with pride, "By the vay, I'm not a brownie, I'm not a stripy. I am a tiger, that's vhat I am, and if you ever cross me, I vill kill you!"

After that, Bohdan walked away and disappeared into the shadows of Mortis Bode, vanishing before Chokka's eyes. Strangely enough, Chokka was filled with pride and took Bohdan's words as the ultimate compliment.

In The Shadows

Chapter VIII
Kimbizi

Every year, the dry season unleashed its merciless wrath. Prey was scarce, the sun was sweltering and the old expression, "Only the strong survive," was never more applicable. Despite the harsh conditions, Bohdan continued to thrive as a solitary predator though his quest for prey of substantial size became more difficult as he traveled to a region of Mortis Bode where foliage, concealment and game were exiguous.

While exploring this new landscape Bohdan happened upon a small pool of water within a secluded cave. Unlike other felids that avoid submerging themselves in water, tigers are adept swimmers and love to lie in pools to cool off, relax and rid themselves of pesky parasites.

Days had passed since Bohdan made a substantial kill. Out of desperation, he decided to venture beyond the confines of Mortis Bode, something he hadn't done since being on his own.

While piercing through the outer edge of the forest into the open plains, Bohdan spotted a small group of rare common eland antelopes in the distance that appeared to be looking in his direction. Because the plains offered no substantial cover or camouflage, Bohdan recognized that his chances of sneaking up on one of them to make a successful kill were slim to none. Therefore, in order to conserve his energy, Bohdan decided to remain steadfast while keeping a watchful eye on their every move.

Hoping for a miracle, he yearned for the elands to saunter in his direction. While fixated on the position of the antelopes, Bohdan spotted movement in his peripheral view. An unknown feline momentarily took his concentration away from the deer-like grass eaters. The feline that had temporarily captured Bohdan's attention was Kimbizi, an attractive female cheetah. Bohdan watched as she began to stalk, something that all predator felids do prior to engaging in a hunt, but he was curious to know her target.

As far as he could see, there was no prey in the immediate vicinity, other than the elands and several impalas, which were hundreds of meters away in the open. Bohdan once again focused his attention on the herbivores, then back on Kimbizi but refused to believe that this feline would attempt to stalk from that great of a distance. Before he could rationalize this strange behavior, Kimbizi dashed toward the impalas like a bolt of lightning, bypassing the eland antelopes that were much closer.

Bohdan had barely risen to focus on the attack but it was all over no sooner than it had begun. All that was left to see was a cloud of dust and the final struggle for life before the impala succumbed to Kimbizi's deadly jaws.

Never having seen a cheetah, Bohdan was astonished at her awesome display of speed and her unique style of hunting. Curious to learn more about this strange feline, Bohdan decided to get a closer look while maintaining his cover. Meanwhile, Kimbizi was exhausted from her kill and tried to catch her breath as she dragged the impala to a secure location to keep from being spotted by larger carnivores.

Unfortunately, the plains were full of opportunistic eyes and none more so than the hyenas, which survived by scavenging whenever possible and stealing prey from smaller hunters. The most ruthless and dominant bunch of hyenas in this region were known as the Swedes. They had a reputation for being wanton killers and had little respect for any animal in their path. Kimbizi was sure that she was being watched and nervously tried to rip open the abdomen of the carcass to gorge in the event she was forced to retreat by an enemy.

Unfortunately, she was too late. The Swedes, led by Halmah, a large female queen, were watching and waiting for the right moment before swarming on the cheetah's location.

Kimbizi spotted the hyenas charging in front of her and then caught a glimpse of other members of their group flanking either side. Survival instincts kicked in and Kimbizi abandoned her kill and withdrew in the opposite direction where the rest of the Swedes were approaching with deadly intentions. Aware that she was literally surrounded and no match for the bone-crushing jaws of a hyena, Kimbizi sprinted to the nearest tree that happened to be a few meters away.

Unless the hyenas had learned how to climb trees, she would be safe until the hyenas depart.

Still in the shadows of Mortis Bode,
Bohdan observed intently as the hyenas harassed his
contemporary and savagely devoured her kill. Minutes
later, the entire carcass was no more and the hyenas were
on their way to terrorize another unsuspecting victim.

Once she was sure that the hyenas were no longer a
threat, Kimbizi descended from the tree. As she dejectedly
walked near the edge of the forest, Bohdan made his
presence known.

"Hel-" was all he could utter before Kimbizi bolted
back across the plains and up the same tree.

Bohdan cautiously walked towards Kimbizi's location
and attempted to assure his interest that he meant no harm,
but an even more cautious Kimbizi was not taking any
chances. She hissed at him violently to scare him away but
the young tiger continued his approach. As Bohdan drew
closer, however, Kimbizi became enthralled, just as others
had by the fascinating conglomerate of stripes and unique
markings that made up his regal appearance. She was
startled by Bohdan's strange but magnificent physique;
after all, that was what had driven her back up the tree in
the first place.

Since leaving the guidance of Chokka three years ago,

Bohdan's physical appearance had changed dramatically. Although still young, he was now six hundred pounds of raw power and continued to grow steadily. Due to the hot climate, his coat had grown scruffy and disheveled around his neck and shoulders. The rest was slick and evenly groomed, which defined his enormous muscular frame. The most unique and daunting element of his physique, other than his huge head and his large pearly incisors, were his abnormally massive shoulders.

Tigers like to conceal their prey therefore, after a kill, they often drag it several meters to a place of comfort and privacy. However, Bohdan had taken this practice beyond his natural instincts. He had continued to do as Chokka taught him and would haul his kills to elevated locations. As a result, his shoulders, forelegs and neck muscles were colossally large, granting him an even more intimidating appearance.

Bohdan reached the base of the tree and looked up at Kimbizi. "I apologize if I startled you. I don't vant to hurt you, I only vant to help."

Kimbizi was still mesmerized by his appearance. She remained silent for a moment before responding in rapid-fire speech.

"I don't know what you are, but if you really want to help, leave me and let me pass!"

Bohdan slowly lowered his head and began to walk away. Because of their size, cheetahs are very wary of other predators but Kimbizi sensed that this stranger was sincere and that she may have been too harsh.

After a moment's hesitation, she called out to Bohdan, *"Hey, slow down; what's your name?"*

Bohdan stopped and turned around to face Kimbizi

"My name is Bohdan."

Still a little winded but confident that he posed no immediate threat, Kimbizi introduced herself.

"I am Kimbizi."

Then, she carefully inched down the tree to inspect the stranger more closely. Once on solid ground, Kimbizi and Bohdan began to circle one another, attentively taking in the other's beauty.

"You're extremely fast," Bohdan said admiringly.

Flattered, Kimbizi responded, *"You really think so? You're probably not too slow yourself."*

Bohdan looked in the direction of the Swedes' departure and asked, "Hoo vere those ruffians and vhy'd they steal your kill?"

"The Swedes, they're very vicious killers. Whatever you do, avoid them. I don't mean to be rude, but you have a curious tongue; where are you from? I have never seen anything like you around here before."

Bohdan replied proudly, "I'm a tiger and I'm not from here."

"Tiger? I've never heard of a tiger before. I'm a cheetah!" To impress him, she bolted away several meters and back in a flash to flaunt her speed.

Before Bohdan could respond, he was distracted by movement in the distance. He spotted a pack of pronghorns at the edge of the plains, which reminded him of the crucial need to satisfy his hunger. His new friend was starving too and had noticed the group as well, but found herself in a precarious dilemma. Although Kimbizi was confident that she could make a successful kill at this distance, she was unsure whether or not the stranger wouldn't take it away from her as the hyenas had earlier.

Bohdan, on the other hand, had a one track mind; FOOD! Without another word, he crouched low to the ground and stealthily slunk through the high grass in the direction of the pronghorns. Kimbizi looked on in awe at the anomalous array of stripes coalescing perfectly with the surroundings, temporarily concealing his threatening presence. Before long, Bohdan was within striking distance. Several of the pronghorns nervously looked in the direction of the threat, innately sensing danger. A couple of scouts carefully scanned the area for any signs of movement.

While one scout made sure to keep his eyes on Kimbizi, another thought he saw something lying still in the high grass and motioned his head forward, straining his eyes to get a better look. After a few intense seconds, the scout dismissed his concerns. As the pronghorns eased their vigilance, Bohdan launched his attack like a young lioness but much faster.

Kimbizi shook her head while thinking, *"He has no chance, he's much too slow."*

Pronghorns are among the fastest land mammals in the world. They often give cheetahs a good race but Bohdan was unaware of this fact. Although tigers are not as fast as cheetahs, their stamina is superior. Bohdan unveiled his lethal blend of grace and power as he sprinted toward his objective. He was eventually spotted by one of the scouts, who initially had been too distracted by Kimbizi to see Bohdan barreling in his direction.

The scout immediately sounded the alarm which caused the herd to scatter. Unfortunately, he was the target of Bohdan's aggression. The scout briefly paused to make sure the entire pack was on the run before abandoning his position in a swift retreat.

The Pronghorn prematurely alternated high jumps between his sprints to show that his speed was superior to his pursuer's, but the tiger remained undaunted by this display and accelerated to a full sprint.

Feeling the thud of the tiger's stride, the frantic pronghorn abandoned his pompous display and attempted to make a last second evasive maneuver. Bohdan, anticipating every move, lunged and was just able to clip the pronghorn from the rear with one of his huge paws.

That was just enough to cause the animal to lose its footing and tumble to the ground.

Bohdan wasted no time reeling in his victim and delivering a crushing bite to the animal's larynx, suffocating it to death. Kimbizi watched in amazement as Bohdan finalized his kill.

After resting for a moment, he brought the carcass back towards Kimbizi and to her surprise, allowed her to eat her fill while he stood guard. After both had eaten, Kimbizi humbly thanked Bohdan for his generosity.

"You're truly amazing!" she exclaimed.

Bohdan replied, "You are pretty amazing as vell."

The cheetah said coyly, *"Hope to see you around again."*

"Perhaps," replied Bohdan.

"Remember, whatever you do, avoid the Swedes; oh, and the Brownbacks too. They are big felids like you and more dangerous than the Swedes."

"I vill do my best," Bohdan assured her. Kimbizi walked away and then looked back just in time to witness Bohdan's silhouette dissolve as he reentered the forest.

In The Shadows

Chapter IX
Magnificent
Migration

The Nomads' pride had changed substantially since Bohdan's departure. The cubs of Catava were now grown and essential members of the pride. Kisa had become an extremely skillful hunter and a favorite among the lionesses. Faraji, by default, was heir to the king's throne and now was the time for him to prove to the elder members of the pride that he was worthy of such a position. Although he had developed the physique of a dominant male, Faraji was lackadaisical about embracing his royal duties and more interested in showing off for the females and bullying the younger males.

Heavy downpours marked the beginning of the rainy season, and with it, the massive migration of the ungulates. Every year, millions of Cape buffalos, zebras, wildebeests and other herbivores journeyed to this part of the region from the cold climate of the north; an indication that the cycle of seasons had been completed.

This gargantuan phenomenon was good news for the carnivores because the herbivores often fell victim to the predators, providing a major source of food. Accompanying this massive gathering was one particular family of Cape buffalos that were extremely aggressive, highly organized and had one agenda every year, to terrorize the lions. These behemoths were fearless when it came to lions and wouldn't hesitate to initiate an attack to protect their members or to convey their dominance. The ill-tempered, well-muscled Cape buffalos weighed roughly two thousand pounds each and were among the largest and most dangerous animals that frequented this region. This group, numbering in the hundreds, was led by their monarch Guarrad, who was one of the most belligerent buffalos of them all.

The deadly rivalry between the buffalos and lions had lasted for generations and until recently, the buffalos had dominated by injuring and killing several lions during the last few migrations. This particular season, King Sayid and the Nomads were at full strength and confident that their imminent battle with the buffalos would result in the Nomads' victory.

The battle would be Faraji's debut as the true beneficiary to the king's throne. In the past, Sayid had been overprotective, adding to the existing tension between the two of them.

Since most of the Nomads still viewed him as a spoiled, uninspired youngster who happened to be the heir to the throne, the king believed that Faraji's participation in their pending conflict with the buffalos would demonstrate to the rest of the pride that he indeed had courage and was worthy of being treated as the rightful successor.

As the rainy season began, the landscape of the region changed from a vast and desolate wasteland to a sea of green grass, foliage and water holes as far as the eye could see. Every resident of this region stood to benefit one way or another from the mass migration of the ungulates but none seemed to benefit more than the giant inhabitants of Crocodile Deep.

The ungulates had to cross the dreaded river to reach the nutrient-enriched grasslands on the other side. In doing so, thousands perished in a spectacular display of savagery and carnage as Crocodile Deep was transformed into a bloody smorgasbord. Hundreds of mammals would be devoured by the crocs each year, enabling the crocodiles to grow to prehistoric sizes.

The Nomads prepared several months in advance for this event in order to seek revenge on Guarrad and his mob of Cape buffalos. Under the leadership of King Sayid, the Nomads had been trampled ever since Guarrad had become the monarch of the testosterone-driven buffalos many years ago. But this season, the king had a battle plan that he hoped would turn the tide in the pride's favor. The only issue that concerned him was Faraji's apathetic attitude.

Sayid looked forward to his offspring proving his value by killing one of the Cape buffalos but was unsure whether the young lion was mentally prepared to do so. If Faraji were to have a plausible chance of bringing down any member of the Guarrad posse, every member of the Nomads must execute his or her predetermined role in the attack to perfection.

The day of the big battle began with a rumble; literally. The ground began to grumble with the steady, nerve rattling vibration of countless heavy hooves as the first drove of ungulates amassed on top of the outer bank. The Nomads had timed the exact arrival of the ungulates perfectly. However, one problem had been unforeseen and unanticipated; the steady downpour of rain, which the lions hated but for which they were nevertheless prepared.

While the rest of the Nomads maintained their positions, King Sayid was stationed on top of a large mound that allowed him to oversee his plan of attack. Just then, he was joined by a familiar flock of Lappet-faced vultures led by Saabir.

The first wave of ungulates began to descend the outer bank of Crocodile Deep, but they were hesitant to cross. Their instincts alerted them to the dangers of the river however they were starving and anxious to arrive at the rich greenery on the other side. Just like the lions, the crocodiles were ready for the ungulates' arrival and were hovering just below the surface of the murky water, waiting on the first victim to enter the kill zone. The backs of some of the larger crocodiles broke the surface of the water causing some members of the first wave who had taken this journey before, to panic and retreat in the opposite direction.

The panicked stampede of thousands of animals fleeing the river's edge created unimaginable chaos just as the second wave of ungulates approached. This group was just as anxious to cross Crocodile Deep and thus had no intention of retreating, resulting in an enormous collision with the first arrivals.

Pandemonium of epic proportions ensued. The momentum of the second wave pushed hundreds of the first wave into the river, provoking the callous crocodiles to immediately begin their gruesome assault. Now that the carnage had begun, the ungulates had no choice but to brave the perilous waters as they rushed to safety on the other side. Thousands survived the trip across, but hundreds were killed by the crocodiles and just as many or more were trampled or drowned from exhaustion.

After several minutes, the river was bloodied throughout and littered with severed limbs, torn flesh and floating carcasses. Hours passed as the migration continued and the crocodiles kept pace by maiming and killing the ungulates with brutal efficiency. The thousands that had already successfully made it across Crocodile Deep began to fill the plains quickly.

Due to the overwhelming rainfall, visibility was limited therefore, King Sayid ordered Saabir and his flock of vultures to take to the skies to locate the Cape buffalos. Sayid watched the vultures intently as they flapped their wings vigorously to shake off as much precipitation as possible, before taking flight under the onslaught of the heavy downpour. Later, when the vultures were high enough to hover over the storm and mostly out of the way of the bombardment of the heavy rain, they scoured the landscape in search of the infamous Guarrad posse.

With the vulture's superior vision, it didn't take long to locate their objective. Saabir led the flock as they uniformly fell in line and formed a large circle formation directly above the buffalos to reveal their exact location. The buffalos hardly noticed the birds hovering above; their only concern was to survive the crossing of Crocodile Deep.

Because they had participated in this mass migration for generations, the Guarrad posse didn't take these prehistoric killers for granted. They carefully watched the crocodiles' behavior and waited patiently until the river's predators had eaten their fill.

Guarrad paid little if any attention to the strange vulture formation high above; his focus was solely on the mayhem taking place in the river below as the crocs continued to ravage the helpless participants of the migration.

He commented sarcastically, "Sacrificial lambs," while surveying the violence with undisguised pleasure.

The Cape buffalos knew that once the crocodiles finished overindulging, they would be virtually inert and less prone to attack. At this point, the remaining ungulates would be able to pass with relative ease.

Several hours had passed before the carnage began to decrease. One by one, the crocs dropped off in exhaustion, satiated with their kills. The Cape buffalos waited patiently for precisely the right moment before scurrying across the dreaded river unscathed. Once on the other side, they regrouped and confirmed that all members of their posse were present. Then, the Guarrad posse began to graze confidently in the middle of the marsh—also the center of the Nomads' trap.

Strategically positioned in the high grass, the Nomads waited patiently under the miserable downpour for King Sayid's command.

As Sayid tried to confirm one last time that his pride was in position, he noticed that the plains were filling up with mammals more quickly than expected. He surmised that the unprecedented crowds might impede the lions' attack and jeopardize the ambush if he didn't act now therefore, to avoid such a catastrophe, King Sayid hurriedly gave his order in the form of a loud but brief roar and the Nomads began their assault.

As the lions charged through the marsh, they triggered a massive stampede that broke out in all directions. Expecting an attack, the Cape buffalos formed a circular shield around the young, the sick, and the elderly.

"Head to higher ground," Guarrad ordered the members of the shield. Then, with just as much determination as contempt, he yelled, "We will take care of these brown backs!"

While Guarrad and his brothers positioned themselves to mount a counterattack, members of the sentinels controlled the massive herd like shepherds as the rest of the pride attempted to separate the weaker buffalos from the heartier and more powerful members.

The lions' strategy seemed to work perfectly initially. Nonetheless, the buffalos promptly turned the tables on King Sayid and his pride as the Guarrad brothers began to bulldoze through the lions' assault. The king watched with concern as several members of his pride were trampled and hurled through the air like weightless sandbags by the mean-spirited buffalos.

Sensing that the buffalos were gaining momentum and confidence with each passing moment, the king gave another order but this time, the vultures were the recipients and responded uniformly.

Numbering in the dozens, they identified their targets and began to nosedive in unison like kamikaze fighters with their powerful, razor-sharp talons ready to dislodge the eyes of the Cape buffalo. The attack was ferocious as the vultures dive-bombed the buffalo with little regard for self-preservation.

Horrified by this blitzkrieg, the buffalos were
overwhelmed and retreated in terror. The vultures' assault
caused the buffalo to break ranks, leaving one of the elderly
members to contend with the Nomads alone.

Faraji seized this moment to prove himself and attacked
the lone buffalo with the utmost ferocity. Cognizant that

this battle would be significant to the young lion's status, the pride pulled back and watched as Faraji attempted to bring down the weak bovine. The young lion put up a valiant effort but the elderly buffalo, although fragile from old age and weakened by the long journey, was not willing to go down without a fight.

Faraji went for his victim's neck but the buffalo was able to hook one of his horns between the top of the lion's foreleg and chest. With one heave of his huge head, the buffalo hurled the heir apparent several feet in the air, ultimately causing Faraji's disgraceful landing in a muddy puddle.

Unwilling to allow their fractious quarry to escape or risk injury to Faraji, the pride launched an intervention led by Jaleel, the dominant guardian. After several minutes, the buffalo succumbed to the four lions on his back and dozens more that yanked and grabbed whatever they could sink their fangs and claws into. Before long, the Nomads were able to expire the stubborn old brute putting an end to his misery.

The Nomads claimed victory but they had paid a heavy price. Many lions labored as they dragged their tired and battle-worn bodies back to the camping ground. Several members had been seriously wounded during the intense battle including Catava who suffered a serious injury to her shoulder. Despite their afflictions, the Nomads celebrated the rare victory over the Cape buffalo.

Once the festivities ceased, the seniors convened secretly for an impromptu meeting. Although several years had passed since Bohdan's departure from the Nomads, the wounds that ensued from his brief stay were still fresh. Many senior members of the pride felt deeply that king Sayid had committed the ultimate betrayal and had come together on many occasions to plot a strategy to exact some form of retribution. Unfortunately, they were never able to agree on a strategy to undermine the king until now. They were pleased with Faraji's efforts against the Cape buffalos; therefore, in Sayid's absence, they unanimously crowned Faraji co-king as a means to finally convey the pride's displeasure of their king's betrayal. Once the king learned about this premature decision, he announced his anger and disagreement with the vindictive decision.

Though Faraji was destined to either become co-king or king in time, king Sayid believed that Faraji had yet to fully prove himself, even though he had demonstrated great courage against the buffalo. His argument was that Faraji was not mentally mature enough for such a position.

The seniors disagreed and refused to vacillate on their decision.

The only way the king could be dethroned was if he voluntarily relinquished his authority or was overthrown by a more powerful and dominant male. None of the seniors thought Faraji was mature enough physically or mentally to overthrow the king, nor did they feel he was truly worthy of being appointed co-king. The decision was clearly made to have a pernicious affect. The seniors believed that by promoting Faraji to such a position, they could take advantage of the tension between him and the king. The co-king would still be required to obey Sayid's commands; however, if he disagreed with the king and had the support of the majority of seniors, Faraji would have more leverage to overrule a decision made by Sayid. In addition, depending on his popularity, if Faraji ever garnered the support of the pride and decided to start one of his own, he would already have a substantial following to do so.

In The Shadows

Chapter X
Outrageous

Miles away, though still within the territorial bounds of the Nomads, Bohdan also awaited the arrival of the mass migration for both obvious and less obvious reasons. He wanted to find his way back to his homeland and believed that one these travelers may provide clues if coerced—but first, he had to satisfy his craving for fresh meat. The migrants littered the plains, grazing the vegetation and pausing frequently at water holes to quench their thirst.

Bohdan watched under the cover of elephant grass as he patiently waited for his opportunity to pounce on unsuspecting prey. The young tiger had never before witnessed an event of such enormity. Awestruck by the sheer size and variety of this massive gathering, Bohdan was unaware that he was slowly and inadvertently being surrounded. His broken outline blended in perfectly with the high grass to such a degree that he went virtually unnoticed by the skittish herd.

Mindful that the herd was oblivious to his position, Bohdan located his target and attacked with celerity reminiscent of Kimbizi.

An unsuspecting adult zebra had managed to meander within several yards of Bohdan's location. As he sprinted after her, the zebra tried to escape by running through the shallow waters to deter her pursuer, but Bohdan raced forward. Unlike lions—who often avoid traveling through water, even when in pursuit of a meal—tigers are fond of it and due to their large, padded paws, they can scamper through shallow waters at extraordinary speeds.

The deadly attack was swift as Bohdan made a spectacular leap midstride with his claws unsheathed. He nearly overshot his target entirely but was able to anchor his claws deep into the zebra's shoulders, momentarily riding on top of its back before toppling over to one side, pulling the zebra to the ground.

A healthy adult zebra is a very powerful animal and not easily taken off its feet by a single predator but Bohdan made his triumph appear routine. The zebra struggled valiantly to regain its footing until its throat was finally collapsed by Bohdan's massive canines.

The sound of the clash caused chaos among the massive herd. As animals began to scatter blindly, the sight of scampering prey instinctively incited Bohdan to give chase. The juvenile tiger abandoned his kill and launched a devastating attack on the fleeing stampede by upending countless members, one by one. He propelled himself recklessly into the charging herd like a renegade torpedo, nearly decapitating his victims by delivering bone crushing bites to the throat and skull.

Bewildered from all the chaos, a young springbuck carelessly ran toward Bohdan's location while he was in the midst of stifling another victim in the shallow waters. Wedged between two bigger mammals blindly heading in the same direction, the springbuck was inadvertently corralled on a path to collide with the very threat he was attempting to elude. At the last instant, he tried to avoid the deadly fangs of the tiger by jumping over him at an exceptional height. Once airborne, the springbuck was well over thirteen feet off the ground, soaring through the air effortlessly. Unfortunately, as the springbuck approached overhead, Bohdan catapulted his massive frame straight up in the air and snared the ill-fated animal in his massive claws.

The momentum of the springbuck, along with the downward force levied by Bohdan's powerful embrace, caused hunter and prey to rotate almost a full 180 degrees in midair. As a consequence, Bohdan was able to slam his victim to the ground and deliver a lethal bite to its skull.

As the plains begin to calm, the aftermath of Bohdan's wrath became abundantly clear. Six adult herbivores lay fatally wounded and there were no animals in the vicinity to question regarding the path to his homeland. Regret washed over him as he surveyed the carnage of his own wanton savagery, while Chokka's voice rang loudly in his mind.

"Never kill more than ya can eat."

Realizing his mistake, Bohdan made a silent vow to control his rage from then on.

The scent and sound of a kill often carries across the plains quickly and this butchery was no exception. Saabir and his flock of vultures circled high above the massacre and waited for the opportunity to descend upon the fallen carcasses. Saabir had witnessed many kills in his long life but none as spectacular as what he had just observed with Bohdan. The vultures were very anxious to eat, but remained cautious of the striped one.

"Whaaat issss thaaat?" Saabir asked, as much to himself as to his flock.

None of them had seen nor heard of such a magnificent beast before or had they?

Saabir remembered the conversation he had with King Sayid years ago, when he had been dispatched to search the edge of Mortis Bode.

"Have you any other news, perhaps of a lioness accompanied by a striped cub in or around the same vicinity?"

Saabir believed this creature could be the striped one that King Sayid had mentioned years ago. His instincts told him to immediately inform the king of this recent discovery, but his stomach forced him to wait for an opportunity to pilfer from one of the carcasses below.

"After all, good information is best delivered with a full stomach," thought Saabir.

Meanwhile, Bohdan's empty belly won the struggle against his shame. He dragged the springbuck across the rugged terrain to a more secluded and shaded area nearby.

All the commotion had not only attracted the vultures, but the Swedes were beginning to advance quickly to the site. Bohdan began to feast on the carcass, while watching the Swedes move closer and closer. The area was littered with five fresh kills to choose, courtesy of Bohdan, but the antagonistic Swedes preferred to steal food and establish their dominance, whenever the opportunity arose.

Now, within several yards of the carnage, the entire clan of hyenas froze simultaneously; staring at Bohdan with curiosity and disbelief. For several moments, the silence among the hyenas was surreal, an event that was just as unusual as the specimen before them.

Once again, empty stomachs overruled reason and the Swedes inched closer. Bohdan continued to feast and remained crouched behind his kill while he stared down the unruly mob with his bright emerald eyes. From a frontal view, the only part of Bohdan visible to the hyenas was the top of his enormous head and the bulge of his massive shoulders.

The hyenas whispered among themselves.

"Look at those stripes."

"He has humps like a camel."

"A what? What is he?"

"Did you say camel?"

"Look at those eyes. He definitely isn't a brownie."

"Maybe he's a sick brownie."

"We've eaten sick brownies, they never look like that."

After moments of hushed consultation, the hyenas became more boisterous as their confidence increased.

Halmah, the queen of the hyenas, spoke first. "Retreat now or feel the wrath of the Swedes!"

A brazen ruckus of laughter erupted from the hyenas in agreement as Bohdan, undeterred, continued to feast on his kill.

"Maybe it doesn't understand," one member of the clan offered.

Halmah responded, "Well, then, whatever it is, it will pay dearly for its ignorance."

She then gave the signal to encircle the strange being. Subordinate hyenas moved in to surround Bohdan, while the queen moved behind the front line of attack to be safeguarded by the lead princess. The Swedes performed this maneuver routinely whenever they encountered resistance. The goal of this tactic was to intimidate the adversary into giving up its meal or position.

The Swedes began to tighten the circle, moving ever so close to their obstinate foe. With each step, Bohdan's appearance and size became more baffling, so they proceeded with caution.

Irritated by the annoying intruders, Bohdan's impatience became apparent. He reared his head to reveal his large, bloody, saber-like fangs and then released a long and menacing bellow that made the ground tremble. The fur-raising tremor cut through the Swedes façade of courage like a hot knife through butter. Bohdan then raised his ears, revealing their characteristic white spots while gradually rotating them from left to right to determine the movement and location of the antagonists to his rear.

At first glance, the hyenas hastily mistook these peculiar spots for eyes and grew alarmed.

"There are eyes in the back of its head," they screamed in unison, backing away in horror.

The hyenas were perplexed, their confidence shaken and their antagonistic assault halted for the moment. Before they could rethink their strategy, Bohdan blasted the hyenas with a thunderous roar that paralyzed the entire clan.

The majority recovered seconds later and managed to scurry recklessly to safety; others were not so lucky. In an instant, Bohdan had leaped over his partially eaten meal and plowed through the dazed mob delivering several swipes to unsuspecting Swedes, killing three along the way and crippling the queen's princess. Now that the path to the queen was cleared, Bohdan pounced, trapping Halmah beneath his massive claws. She begged for her life now that the circumstances had dramatically changed and she was face to face with her newly discovered worst nightmare.

Bohdan lowered his face mere centimeters from Halmah's. At this distance, she noticed how the sunlight ominously danced around his emerald irises.

"Your tyranny has no place here, do you understand?" Bohdan warned.

"Yes, yes, I do, I do," Halmah fearfully barked.

"Cross my path no more!"

Halmah could only nod her head rapidly in agreement.

"Leave!" Bohdan roared angrily.

He had killed too many that day and mercifully allowed Halmah to recover and corral the remainder of her severely wounded clan. Several meters away, Saabir and crew were also recovering from the paralyzing shockwave of Bohdan's roar. With a few less feathers, the vultures hastily abandoned their meal and took flight to inform King Sayid of this petrifying encounter.

Chapter XI
Haunted & the
Hunted

It was midday and the Nomads were lounging around as they regularly did during the day and especially after consuming a meal.

Suddenly, Saabir and his crew began to descend on the location of the Nomads where King Sayid was accompanied by Faraji and Jaleel. The three lions watched with amazement as the vultures touched down uniformly, one by one, like a squadron of jet fighters landing on an aircraft carrier. Although Saabir had a close relationship with the King, out of respect and as a precautionary measure, he often touched down several meters away whenever he approached the pride.

Normally, Saabir arrived solo but this time, the entire flock was in tow. King Sayid unhurriedly rose and began to approach Saabir alone as the rest of the pride, at least those who were awake and aware of the vultures' presence—looked on with curiosity.

Sayid spoke first, "To what do I owe the honor of the entire multitude?"

Saabir responded as he bowed to the king, "Theee hhonnorrr issss ouurrrsssss."

He then cleared his throat and continued slowly. "Aahemm. Weee brrrriinggg yyoou newwwsss offff the sssstrrriiiipddd onne. Heee exxisssttssss beeeeyyyonnddd tthe marrrrsssshyyy prrrovinncce. Heeee issss lllittllle nooo mmmoorre. Wwweee hhavvve fffeeeasstedd hheavvillyy off caarrcassssesss hee haass ssslllaainn."

Sayid was stunned to hear that Bohdan had survived Mortis Bode. He briefly reflected on the turmoil he had brought to the pride years ago by allowing Bohdan to live. He was also reminded of the loss of his queen, Malika and his dear friend and guardian, Zihad.

"Tell me more," the king demanded quietly as he intently stared at his messenger.

"Alllll duue theee hhonorssshipppp oofff yoourrrsssselfff aandd yourrr ppriiiddde, Iiii hhhavvve ssseeeeeennn sssstrrrangge fffeeeellinnnesss iinn mmmyy Eeyyeesss, noooo irrrrevvvverrrrennncce tooo yyourrr hhonnorr, bbutt tthisss bbeeassst iisss thhe ssstrrannggesst, mmmossst ffforroociiousss, mmmosst mmmagnniffficenntt ssssollittarryy ssslaaayerrr Iii hhavve evvverrr wwwitnnessssed —and hiiis rrrooaar!"

Arrogantly, Sayid interjected Saabir mid sentence, "Understand this. My kind is the mightiest of all felines. Furthermore, your allegiance is with the Nomads, not that freak of nature who dares to intrude on my territory or have you forgotten that?"

Taken aback, Saabir calmly leaned his head to one side, opening and closing his beak before responding. He stared directly into the tumultuous eyes of the king and took one step backwards as his entire flock took one step forward simultaneously.

Saabir's voice was now bold but still creaky and slow as he stated, "Alllll duue rrevverrencce tooo yyourrr hhonnorrsshippp, hhhavvve yyoou foorrgottenn the biigg hhornns or Guuurrraaddss, aasss yyoou preeefferr? Mmyy allliaancce isss wwwithh yyoou, yoourr hhonorsssshipppp bbutt mmyy allleegiancce isss wwwith tthhosse that acccommpannyy mee and tooo theem, Ii amm sserrrvedd. Fforrggive mee, yoourr hhonorsssshipppp ffoorr iinnjjectttingg mmyy vviewwss. Yyoou aarre sstiilll the miighttieesstt oofff kiinnggsss."

Sayid answered peremptorily, "Until further notice, report any sightings of this intruder immediately. He must be dealt with!"

Saabir nodded in agreement. "Cconsidderr itt ddonne, yoourr hhonorssshipppp."

Saabir took a couple steps forward, performed a left face as if he were a soldier executing a squad drill, then with a running start followed by two hops on one leg, he took flight. The rest of the flock repeated this maneuver as they broke formation one after the other to become airborne.

King Sayid stood motionless as he watched Saabir's crew fly away. He was pondering how to deal with this dilemma without informing the others that the striped one lived.

Weeks had passed since the Nomads' encounter with the Cape buffalo. The embattled lions still remained the most dominant pride in the region based on numbers alone. However, their ability to defend that honor against a formidable foe was questionable. Key members of the pride were still recovering from injuries suffered in the brutal battle. Kisa, a superb lioness, and Jaleel, unquestionably the most intimidating male of the pride, were among the few that were virtually unscathed during the battle. Jaleel and his brother Jelani were the only two dominant guardians left that were most loyal to King Sayid. Neither had the bloodline to officially become king, but based on the size and youth of Jaleel, the more dominant of the two siblings, there would be no formidable opponent to combat his authority, if he ever had aspirations to become king.

At first glance, Jaleel could easily be mistaken for the pride's king because of his size and peculiar mane. It covered nearly sixty percent of his back, chest and abdomen, granting him an intimidating appearance common to kings.

Luckily for Sayid, Jaleel was content with being the head guardian for now.

King Sayid had been preoccupied with the news of Bohdan's existence for several days. He eventually hatched a clandestine plan that he hoped would eliminate Bohdan once and for all and for the sake of his throne.

The king secretly summoned Jaleel. Sayid's most trustworthy guardian was tasked to seek and destroy the striped one before the seniors or any other members became aware of his continued existence. The king knew that the striped one would be no match for Jaleel and any distant memory of the interloper's existence would soon be lost forever.

The rest of the pride was unaware of his mission but Jaleel's prolonged absences were bound to raise suspicion. After all, he was the primary guard and chief protector of the king. Eventually, the pride would grow curious as to his whereabouts. Although Sayid was not the most typical king, he was quite clever. He used the seniors' ill-timed decision to appoint Faraji as the co-king to his advantage. Sayid relinquished most of his duties to Faraji to avert attention from Jaleel. This proved to be unsettling for the seniors in particular, because they were now forced to become more involved to ensure Faraji was making the right decisions for the pride, in the event he became king.

Chapter XII
Infrasonically
Speaking

Near the outskirts of Mortis Bode, Bohdan rested near the mouth of a small cave embedded in a mountainous cliff that overlooked the forest. He had just finished eating his fill of a kudu carcass and was drifting lazily to sleep.

Suddenly, he was jarred to full awareness by the strangest sensation. In the distance, an unfamiliar but distinct cry of agony was heard in a way that he had never experienced. It was as though he could feel the cries of anguish, rather than hear them. Bohdan's curiosity demanded that he investigate this strange phenomenon.

As Bohdan stealthily maneuvered down the steep and rocky terrain, he noticed the unfamiliar cries for help were rejoined by an even more distant bawl of distress. While Bohdan sought the source of these disturbances, his ears began to pick up the sounds of an intense struggle between an unfamiliar beast and the recognizable prattle of those that were known to him.

The struggle seemed to intensify with each passing moment. The sound of brush being thrashed and limbs being broken grew louder as Bohdan gradually approached the unseen battle.

Concealed by the darkness, in addition to his unique camouflage, Bohdan laid low as the ruckus was finally revealed in its entirety. Bursting into view with the aid of the bright moon light came one of the strangest animals that Bohdan had ever seen.

The large beast, with a thick, snake-like nose, plowed through the brush, begging for help from his mother as he was viciously attacked by a pack of hyenas. Having seen enough, Bohdan immediately made his presence known with a deafening roar, paralyzing the hyenas in the midst of their assault. The seismic shock of Bohdan's horrifying roar caused the hyenas to stumble to the ground, as they momentarily lost control of all bodily functions.

The big beast, awestruck at the sight of the weirdest feline that he had ever fixed his eyes upon, stopped abruptly in his tracks. Bohdan and this beast, a juvenile

African elephant known as Abdulah, stared motionlessly at one another while the hyenas regained consciousness and scurried away into the concealment of the thick brush.

An embattled Abdulah spoke, while he attempted to catch his breath and contain his crying.

Between sniffles, he said gratefully, "You saved me, and-and you-you speak my language!"

Not only is the roar of a tiger paralyzing, its stifling bellow, laced with low frequency infrasound is similar to the communicative aspects of the sounds made by elephants and dolphins.

Abdulah cocked his head to one side with curiosity; his long trunk swaying like a pendulum. Bohdan continued to stare at this bizarre, frightened animal without giving any response.

"My name is Abdulah. What's yours?"

The scowl on Bohdan's face relaxed as he responded shortly. "Bohdan!"

Suddenly, Bohdan turned his attention to the path from which Abdulah had come. He again felt a vibrating sensation of hearing through feeling. This time, the powerful, low frequency infrasound that Bohdan sensed grew stronger.

"Abdulah! Abdulah, baby, where are you? Are you OK?"

The frantic cry was repeated a couple more times, before the ground beneath Bohdan's feet began to shake violently, disturbing the branches on nearby vegetation. Abdulah interpreted this silent call and responded with a low rumble in the same unfamiliar manner.

"Mama, I'm OK. I'm over here."

Immediately after Abdulah's response, the shaking of the ground intensified as the sounds of disturbed shrubbery and breaking tree limbs grew nearer. Seconds later, the bright moon revealed the largest animal that Bohdan had ever seen, a full-grown African matriarch elephant standing eleven feet tall, known as Nazya, who happened to be Abdulah's hysterical mother.

As soon as he saw his mother, Abdulah trumpeted joyfully and ran to greet her, while yelling, "Mama, Mama, he saved me. He saved me!"

Nazya immediately embraced Abdulah with her massive trunk, but before she could respond, she noticed the presence of the most bizarre feline that she had ever come across. She abruptly unleashed a thunderous trumpet, followed by a long, menacing bellow that emphatically said, "Get away from my young one, demon!"

Bohdan's eyes took in the thick ivory tusks and the huge, wing-like ears. He was extremely curious of this creature. Nazya then displayed a mock charge, kicking up debris and waving her enormous tusks and trunk up and down to show that she meant business. Dodging her huge trunk, Abdulah tried to intervene.

"No, Mama, no, he saved me! He saved me, Mama!" Bohdan, on the other hand, was not intimidated by Nazya's size, nor her act of aggression. He responded just as forcefully with a mock charge of his own and a thunderous roar simultaneously.

"I'm no demon, I am a tiger!"

Nazya got an uncomfortable eyeful of Bohdan's saber tooth incisors and his emerald green eyes, which reflected the moonlight as though they were two laser pointers. She immediately realized that this strange being had no intention to obey her admonition. Startled by the strange one's defiance and the fact that she was able to understand his response infrasonically, she took several steps backwards as she pulled Abdulah closer with her huge trunk.

Abdulah tried to allay her fears. "Mama, Mama, listen—what I'm trying to tell you is he saved my life and he speaks our language, the language of mammalians. His name is Bohdan."

Nazya continued to stare down at Bohdan intently, while maintaining a tight grip on Abdulah. She took a step forward while unleashing another seismic growl.

"If what Abdulah says is true, how can I honor your favor?"

Bohdan responded, "I seek the land of vhite powder, the land of vinter's fury; do you know of such a place?"

"Perhaps you seek the domain of Amur, which is several Eyes away. To get there, you must follow the Eye of dawn."

Bohdan bowed his head humbly, grateful for the information.

Abdulah asked, "Can we go with Bohdan, Mama?"

Nazya didn't answer. Her eyes remained fixated on Bohdan. She was not only taken aback that this strange feline was able to speak her language, she was also in awe of his fascinating appearance and fearlessness. Additionally, Nazya was curious to know this strange being's motives. After all, he had saved her young from a clan of bloodthirsty hyenas, but for what reason. Bohdan was mutually inquisitive about the colossal beasts before him. He continued to take in Nazya's trunk, her massive tusks and those enormous ears.

Abdulah broke the staring contest between Nazya and Bohdan with a subtle call to his mother, which prompted Nazya to nudge Abdulah indicating it was time to go. Abdulah glanced at the tiger once more with an expression of longing and gratitude, before leading the way into the dark shadows of Mortis Bode.

Nazya, although grateful, remained wary of Bohdan's presence. She slowly backed away and kept her eyes glued to him for a few paces, before finally turning to follow her calf into the darkness.

In The Shadows

Chapter XIII

Apex

The sun was slowly sinking, casting brilliant blues, reds and purples across the sky. It was time to hunt and Faraji was in charge of orchestrating the attack. The hunt was successful and the Nomads were pleased. They returned to the resting grounds in a fairly festive mood, except for Kisa. She was vying to take over as the lead lioness but she had been slightly injured in the hunt. Instead of lounging around as usual after a successful hunt, Kisa decided to take a walk to ease her pain.

Lionesses normally do not venture too far away from their pride for safety reasons, but on this particular evening, a peculiar smell caught her attention. As a result, Kisa strayed far beyond the security of the pride. She sniffed the air inquisitively and trudged on to establish the source of the peculiar scent she had been following.

A bush had been territorially marked, but its scent was intermingled with a fresh, new, yet familiar odor. This one belonged to Jaleel, who had been absent from the pride for a couple of days now. Realizing that she had strayed an uncomfortable distance from safety, Kisa was relieved that Jaleel was nearby and curious to know where he had been lately.

Several kilometers away, Jaleel was on the trail of the same peculiar scent and hoped it was that of the striped one. However, there was a problem; the scent led into Mortis Bode, a place that was forbidden, even for the "King of the Jungle."

Erect in his posture, Jaleel cautiously approached the outer edge of Mortis Bode. Only a few meters in, the freshly killed carcass of an adult zebra was discovered and marked by the scent the guardian had been tracking. Jaleel instantly became uneasy that such a fresh kill was not crawling with scavengers. He also noticed that the dead zebra had been dragged from a long distance based on the trail left behind it; an enormous feat for an animal that size.

As Jaleel turned around and exited the forest to survey the surrounding area, he observed that his every move was being watched by a myriad of locals. A large audience of herbivores was gathering and jockeying for a clear line of sight off in the distance, as well as a congregation of fowl that began to circle high above, anticipating the inevitable.

Jaleel ignored the onlookers while a light breeze emerged, seemingly grooming his mane as he contemplated whether to continue his quest into Mortis Bode. Meanwhile, Bohdan was returning to his kill after sating his thirst from a nearby water hole. He immediately picked up the scent of the intruder through an action called flehmen. This is a behavior in which a tiger hangs out its tongue, simulating a grimace, to draw smells from the air into specialized organs located in the roof of the mouth to help determine friend from foe.

After assessing the threat, Bohdan confirmed that there was indeed an enemy in the midst. He announced his anger with a series of growls that reverberated throughout Mortis Bode, frightening some of the locals while immediately capturing Jaleel's attention. He saw movement through the foliage but had yet to get a clear visual of the owner of the daunting bellow.

Slowly emerging from the shadows of Mortis Bode, the green of Bohdan's emerald eyes were barely visible in his menacing scowl as his enemy gradually sauntered into focus.

Because these were two dominant males determined to solidify their supremacy, this would surely be an inhospitable encounter. As soon as these elite combatants came in view of one another, without hesitation, they simultaneously unleashed thunderous roars as they charged at each other with blind fury.

At seven hundred pounds of pure muscle and aggression, Bohdan outweighed Jaleel by nearly two hundred pounds and the collision favored him as he plowed into Jaleel like a battering ram.

Jaleel toppled over from the overwhelming impact as Bohdan ripped a mouthful of mane from his throat. Temporarily dazed, Jaleel quickly recovered and barely avoided another vicious attempt by Bohdan to bite through his mane by pushing him off with his thick, muscular hindquarters. Momentarily distracted, Bohdan shook his head to rid his mouth of the huge bundle of hair.

Jaleel immediately tried to take advantage of his opponents brief lapse by delivering a strike of his own with his powerful forelegs. However, Bohdan was fierce and the assault was thwarted. He effortlessly evaded the lion's slow, but potentially deadly attack and quickly countered with two crushing blows of his own with lightning speed, dislodging massive amounts of mane and flesh in the process.

Jaleel attempted to answer with a wild swing that only disturbed the air above Bohdan's head. Quick-witted, Bohdan's reflexes were lightning fast, enabling him to easily evade his opponent's inferior assaults. Like a seasoned pugilist, Bohdan countered with a flurry of devastating combinations to Jaleel's head with his massive claws ripping deep into the cheek and nose area.

The ravaging strikes caused Jaleel to buckle and bleed severely. The lion staggered as he tried to regroup, but the tiger's ferocity and skills as a supreme fighter proved to be too much to handle. Bohdan was merciless in his onslaught, attacking at all angles, keeping the guardian off balance and on the defensive. Jaleel was thoroughly beaten and exhausted. He made one last effort to mount an offensive, but Bohdan reared up on his hindquarters and surged forward, smothering the lion's assault with his broad shoulders. He then delivered successive strikes to Jaleel's head with his unsheathed claws, ripping into his opponents hide with each blow as the lion was driven backwards by the relentless bombardment.

Nearby, Kisa heard the deafening ruckus of the battle and rushed to investigate. Through the cloud of dust and debris, Kisa saw Jaleel fighting desperately to escape the deadly wrath of his opponent. Jaleel was literally defenseless as Bohdan delivered a final multitude of concussive wallops that sent the demoralized guardian tumbling backwards onto his back.

Before Jaleel could recover from his vulnerable position, Bohdan went in for the kill, attacking from a side mount position to evade the lion's powerful hindquarters. Realizing that Jaleel was in peril, Kisa quickly rushed to intervene. Just as Bohdan was about to deliver a fatal bite through Jaleel's thick mane, she hurried over with her head down in a submissive manner and administered a quick, deliberate swipe against one of Bohdan's hindquarters.

This distracted him just enough to allow Jaleel to escape from certain death. An enraged Bohdan snapped his head around to identify the interference. He noticed a female lion, who was down on her belly in a submissive posture to show she was not a threat.

Meanwhile, bloodied, disheveled and severely injured, Jaleel stumbled to his paws. As a guardian, he was trained to fight to the death to protect his honor as well as any member of the pride. Before Bohdan could respond to Jaleel's act of valor, Kisa shouted.

"Bohdan, it's me, Kisa!"

Bohdan's countenance changed in an instant. Excitedly, he asked, "Kisa?!"

Bohdan chuffed as they rubbed their necks together to show familiarity.

"Stop!" Kisa yelled, turning her attention to Jaleel as he gathered his bearings for another futile clash with his opponent.

Blood was dripping puddles from Jaleel's mouth and face as he responded through ragged breaths, "This … intru-der … must die. I … have my … orders!"

Kisa stepped between the two combatants and shouted, "Orders?! What are you talking about? What orders?" Suddenly, she gasped with understanding and disgust. "Ugh, my father put you up to this!"

Jaleel stood silently in disgrace. Not only had he failed his mission, he had mistakenly revealed the king's secret.

Sympathetic to Jaleel's current condition, Kisa addressed him regally. "Despite my disappointment in you and the decision of my father, I will not allow you to throw your life away."

An ungrateful Jaleel grunted through clenched fangs, "You are aware that your irrational affinity towards this intruder is punishable by death?"

Now angry, Kisa raised her voice. "YOU are NOT in any condition to cast judgment upon MY decision and if I were you, I would leave now to save what LITTLE honor you have left."

"Hmmph. The king will know of your treachery," Jaleel boastfully stated.

Kisa gave Jaleel a sarcastic smile as she assessed the damage inflicted by Bohdan and confirmed, "It appears that my treachery will not be the only thing of which my father will be made aware."

Dejected, Jaleel turned and slowly limped back toward the location of the pride.

Excited to see her long lost friend, Kisa turned her attention back to her buddy.

"Bohdan, I can't believe it's you! We thought you were dead when the carcass of Omar was discovered. What of

Malika?"

Bohdan answered by lowering his head to convey that Malika had perished. Kisa paused to show her condolences but then quickly changed the subject.

"Bohdan, look at you! You are magnificent and your stripes are even more amazing than I remember."

Bohdan blushed a little. "You, uh, look ... ahhh," he stumbled in a loss for words.

Playfully, Kisa interjected while posing for each word of choice to describe herself: "Beautiful, awesome, dazzling, like a princess?"

Bohdan agreed; emerald eyes flickering. "Yes and much more."

Then, Kisa blushed and changed the conversation to the serious situation that occurred moments ago. She surveyed the mane and blood that blanketed the ground where Bohdan and Jaleel fought.

"Wow, you really let Jaleel have it! You've just defeated our top guardian! My father will not be pleased and will surely send others to retaliate."

Bohdan responded defiantly, "Let them come!"

Enthralled, Kisa paused momentarily as she and Bohdan stared into each other's souls. He allowed his mind to wonder and contemplated how this land would be with him as king and Kisa by his side. They would rule unchallenged for years and their offspring would be a formidable combination of two supreme specimens of their respective species.

The fantasy was quickly extinguished, however, when Kisa spoke.

"The pride will come looking for me shortly."

Bohdan nodded his head in agreement.

She then asked, thoughtfully, "What will become of you?"

"I'm in search of my home."

Kisa replied, "If you are unsuccessful, promise me that you will return."

Without giving Bohdan a chance to respond, Kisa unexpectedly gave him a quick nuzzle and then trotted off in the direction of the pride.

Chapter XIV
Rebel Yell

Jaleel had taken a detour on his way back to the pride. The deviation from his usual path allowed him to ponder his future with the Nomads and nurse his wounds, both physical and emotional, after being devastatingly trounced by Bohdan.

Meanwhile, Kisa rushed back to camp, hoping to learn more about her father's failed mission to vanquish her cub hood friend. Upon entering the camp, Kisa was immediately confronted by Faraji, who was beginning to grow concerned regarding his sister's whereabouts.

"Kisa, where have you been?"

But Kisa ignored his question and quickly absorbed the mood of the pride. Most of the lions were too lazy to notice her return but Kisa took no chances and quickly ushered

Faraji a safe distance away from the pride to ensure their conversation would be private.

She asked in a hushed tone, "Listen, Faraji, I need you to tell me the truth, are you aware that Bohdan is still alive?"

Faraji was surprised and responded accordingly. "WHAT?! The snakaphant is still alive? That can't be!"

Realizing that her brother's reaction was genuine, Kisa immediately restrained Faraji to keep him from garnering attention and responded with controlled excitement.

"Shhh, keep it down! Yes, it's true. He survived Mortis Bode!"

"How do you know of this?"

Kisa answered in a manner that showed Faraji she still harbored lingering affection for Bohdan.

"Let's just say that I have seen him with my own eyes."

Faraji shrugged away from Kisa angrily. "Your renewed empathy toward this striped pariah will not be tolerated! As your elder, I demand that you tell me his location immediately."

"H-how dare you?" Kisa spit back, "You are my big brother but I will not be forced to reveal a thing until I find out why Jaleel was sent to kill him. And, he is not a pariah!

He's Bohdan!"

King Sayid looked up from the small mound where he was resting. He observed the private clash among his two favorite offspring and decided to investigate but before he could meander over, he noticed that Faraji had suddenly turned his gaze toward a crumpled up mass in the distance.

Faraji was befuddled by Kisa's allegations but the sight of Jaleel laboring to return to the camp caused him to refocus his attention for the moment. Others began to notice Jaleel and in a matter of seconds, the entire pride was on high alert. Several members of the pride rushed to his assistance, including his brother Jalani. The mere sight of Jaleel, demoralized and severely wounded, put the pride in a momentary state of shock as they tried to fathom the inconceivable. Subordinate sizzies and guardians were asked to stand guard as the seniors discussed the cause of Jaleel's condition.

Once he settled into camp and the pride was assured that there was no imminent threat, Jaleel informed the remaining members of the pride that Bohdan was still alive and that he, the defeated guardian, had failed to vanquish the abomination. The seniors were very disturbed that they had not been advised of King Sayid's secret mission to destroy the outcast, even though they would have unanimously supported it. They were even more disturbed to learn that the striped one had survived Mortis Bode.

One senior, after reviewing the injuries Jaleel had sustained, inquired nervously as he looked around as if he was in a state of paranoia. "How many demons were in this clan that attacked you?"

Jaleel humbly responded while he lowered his head in shame. "There was no clan, there was only one."

The seniors, all wide-eyed, gasped in disbelief that any single felidae, other than an extraordinary dominant lion of greater strength and fighting ability, could do such damage to a supreme specimen like Jaleel. Seeing the faces of incredulity among his pride, King Sayid voiced his anger and tried to reassure them that they were superior and second to none.

"We are Lions! We are the kings of all the felidae!" he roared.

But the rest of the pride, though outwardly enthusiastic, questioned the king's claims of supremacy, especially after seeing the damage inflicted on arguably the most dominant lion in the region, let alone the pride.

Faraji selfishly turned his fear and insecurity into feelings of betrayal that his father had not entrusted him to deal with the striped one.

He lashed out, "Father, how could you? Assigning a guardian a task that belongs to a royal?"

"Faraji, my son, you don't understand."

Faraji interrupted the king mid-sentence. "You've always trusted inferior blood over me!"

Before King Sayid could respond, Jaleel raised his head to angrily interject, "How dare you ridicule me, you sizzy!" As he took a step in Faraji's direction, Sayid turned to Jaleel and calmly stated, "Ignore his youthful ignorance, my friend."

Disrespected by Jaleel's remarks and his father's condescension, Faraji's rage boiled over. He attacked without warning, striking out at the unsuspecting guardian but Jaleel was in fact prepared for the surprise attack. The guardian blocked the swipe with his injured shoulder and countered with a powerful blow that found its mark against Faraji's face. Faraji stumbled backwards but before the seniors could intervene, Jaleel pounced and pinned Faraji to the ground.

"The next time you look into my eyes will be your last, little kitty!" Jaleel growled, peering into the fearful, immature soul of Faraji.

King Sayid roared above the fray to maintain order. "Enough!"

However, the damage had already been done. Jaleel dismounted Faraji and with Jalani by his side, turned and walked away from the pride for good, leaving the bystanders stunned.

Even worse, as King Sayid attempted to persuade Jaleel and Jalani to stay, Saabir swooped down from the skies above with news of greater concern.

Earlier, just before dawn, Saabir and his crew had been leisurely mastering the art of riding the wind currents. It was then that they had spotted two large animals below underneath a transparent blanket of mist, thrashing and kicking up foliage in an apparent fit of rage. At first glance, they had perceived the two large animals to be sparring for dominance.

However, as Saabir zoomed in from hundreds of feet above for a closer look at this commotion, he confirmed that the sources of this disturbance had been none other than Guarrad and one of his cantankerous brothers, Gibral.

Saabir immediately abandoned his activities to warn King Sayid of the intruding buffalos.

Unaware of the reason behind Saabir's visit and furious over the recent events, King Sayid snapped, "Your presence is not welcome at this time!"

Saabir kept his distance, but did not fly away. "I will not warn you again my friend. Flee with your life or else," admonished the king.

Saabir took heed to Sayid's warning, but before he turned to take flight, he answered in true vulture form.

"I wiiilll hhonnnorrr yoourr wwisshh, bbutt the onne yyoou knnooww aasss Gguuurradd wwill nnott bee sssoo eeeasssilllyy pperrssuadedd."

In The Shadows

Chapter XV
Buffalo Soldiers

The news of Guarrad's return could not have arrived at a worse time. The majority of the pride was still recovering from recent injuries, in addition to the resignations of Jaleel and Jalani, two key members of the pride.

For the first time in his reign, King Sayid was greatly concerned about the future of the Nomads. He was well aware that a major assault in the near future would surely have catastrophic consequences. While the king contemplated the impending threat from his greatest nemesis, the seniors began to voice their concerns among themselves.

"What are we going to do? We are no match for the Guarrads without the winged ones; we must retreat."

Now recovered from his close encounter with Jaleel, a disillusioned Faraji regrouped and worsened the situation with his poor attitude and sarcasm.

"Yes, Father. What will we do now? Guarrad is on his way and the pariah you failed to kill still haunts us. If I were king, I would have eliminated that freakish beast and destroyed the Guarrads long ago."

Frustrated by Faraji's foolishness, King Sayid gave his heir an earful and backed him into submission.

"Say another word and I will slay you myself! You ask what we will do. This is what we will do! We will fight the Guarrads to the death and afterwards, if you survive, you will have the inevitable task of dealing with Jaleel and the striped one as you see fit, whether you want to or not!"

The king's words left Faraji humiliated and apprehensive of his fate.

Sayid then called the entire pride to attention.

"We will not retreat and we don't need any flying fowl to fight our battles. We are lions! We are the kings of this domain and we will defend it to our deaths!"

He ordered the seniors to gather the healthiest members of the pride to prepare for battle against the buffalos. Despite their resentment toward the king, the seniors were aware that the pride had to unite in order to defeat the threat presented by the buffalos.

Several weeks had passed since the epic battle between the Nomads and the buffalos during the migration. Stung by their defeat and the loss of one of their own, Guarrad was intent upon seeking revenge. He was enraged that the Nomads had not fought fairly, employing the savagely, vicious vultures that sealed the buffalos defeat.

Still incensed, Guarrad ordered two of his three brothers to continue south against their will. He needed them to stay with the rest of the herd, while he and Gibral headed back to retaliate against the pride. He wanted to catch the lions by surprise and kill as many of them as possible.

The two brothers made their way toward the resting grounds of the Nomads, thrashing aggressively through some of the tall grass and sometimes stopping to spar violently against one another. This was how they would excite each other to prepare for an impending battle.

As the brothers made their way past the outer edge of Mortis Bode, Gibral was the first to notice a strange, abnormally large feline emerging from the forest a few meters ahead.

Soon, Guarrad became aware of Bohdan's presence and motioned to Gibral to halt while they analyzed the tiger's body language to determine his motive. Unbeknownst to the two goliaths at large, Bohdan was cognizant of their intrusion before he nonchalantly made his presence known. Luckily for them, he was not interested in prey at the moment.

This day just happened to be the day that Bohdan decided to leave Mortis Bode forever. He was in pursuit of what Nazya, the elephant, referred to as the Amur domain, his true home. After closely monitoring the tiger's behavior, the buffalos determined that the strange feline was not interested in their presence and therefore didn't appear to be a threat at the moment.

Insulted, Gibral commented, "All must pay for their stench of arrogance, including this strange one."

Guarrad, however, having had many encounters with big felines, was not so sure about this enigma. Besides, he was focused on his vengeance against the lions. As Bohdan continued to walk nonchalantly in the opposite direction, Guarrad answered his brother.

"He is strange indeed but he is of no concern to us. Conserve your exuberance and rage for the Nomads!"

Gibral snorted loudly and stared angrily at the departing feline.

"Do you smell that, brother? It's the rancid odor of felinian arrogance. From this day forward, our wrath will be unleashed on all who cross our path, starting with this imbecile!"

Without much more prodding, Guarrad quickly fell under the spell of his brother's aggressive outlook and enthusiasm. They began to charge Bohdan, with the quicker Gibral leading the way.

Meanwhile, Bohdan's thoughts remained focused on leaving the place where he had grown up but still felt so foreign.

Suddenly, the rumbling ground beneath his paws caught his attention. Bohdan turned and was surprised to see the Cape buffalo that he had ignored, thundering wildly in his direction. Furious at this blatant provocation, Bohdan stood his ground.

Throughout the animal kingdom, there is no greater rage than that of a provoked tiger, which many have seen but few have survived.

With his mouth agape, his ears pointing backwards and his tail swinging deliberately side to side, Bohdan was ready to confront the four thousand pounds of aggression.

Guarrad attempted to catch up to his faster, adrenaline filled brother to present a united and intimidating show of force. Finally reaching Gibral's flank, Guarrad happened to noticed a familiar pattern of brown silhouettes approaching from several meters beyond Bohdan's rear.

Before he could visually identify the figures, his keen sense of smell determined that the new arrivals were none other than the Nomads. Now that Guarrad had the Nomads within his sight, his overwhelming yearning for revenge took over. At the last moment, his intentions were to abort the insignificant attack on the strange feline and attack the Nomads instead.

However, before his sudden change in strategy, Guarrad and Gibral had been nearly side by side, blazing toward an unwary foe. Gibral lowered his massive horns to gore the audacious tiger, but Bohdan was prepared for battle. He temporarily incapacitated the buffalo brothers with a ground shaking roar before narrowly evading Gibral's deadly horns by leaping over the buffalo's head.

Stunned, the two behemoths toppled to the ground, creating a massive pair of elongated craters in the soft soil and foliage. Gibral suffered the worst during the violent tumble as his massive horns dug deep into the earth and forced his immense body to flip over to a slow yet painful halt.

Shaking off the instinctive fear that had arisen with Bohdan's roar, the dazed buffalos staggered back to their hooves. Before Gibral could clear his vision and horns of the muddy soil and debris, Bohdan viciously attacked.

He plowed hard into Gibral, while biting and holding on to his snout, sinking his powerful canines deep into the huge herbivore's skull. While attempting to gather his bearings and focus on the Nomads, Guarrad was startled by the horrific sound and savagery of Bohdan's attack on his brother.

Still disoriented, his immediate response was to retreat. Unfortunately for the lions, who had momentarily ceased their approach as they watched the ensuing battle, Guarrad retreated in their direction which prompted the Nomads to scatter wildly in panic.

Guarrad was so engrossed by vengeance that he temporarily forgot all about his brother and continued his pursuit, hoping that any member of the Nomads would be brave enough to take him on. The frenzied lions hastily dashed those hopes by using their greater speed and stamina to avoid any possibility of being gored by the fuming buffalo. Their sole strategy was to distract Guarrad with futile chases, so he would not invade their resting grounds, where the injured and young lay defenseless.

In his pointless attempts to confront the lions, Guarrad made an uncharacteristically perceptive observation; although the lions made sure to keep their distance, it was evident that his threat alone, though respected, wasn't worthy of their undivided attention.

Only then did Guarrad realize that his unsuccessful quest for vengeance may have yielded a bigger loss, one that he would regret for the rest of his life. He turned around immediately to identify what had demanded the lions' curiosity and was stunned by what he saw.

In the distance, the deadly embrace between tiger and buffalo was on full display. Guarrad heard the lone cry of anguish as his brother Gibral desperately fought for his life. Bohdan's powerful jaws were still clamped around Gibral's snout like a vise-grip. Bleeding profusely and fighting with every ounce of energy that remained, Gibral lunged forward sporadically, attempting to trample his attacker to force the release of his death grip.

With a foreleg over the top of one of Gibral's massive horns and the other wrapped underneath the buffalo's throat for added leverage, Bohdan was able to dodge Gibral's powerful hooves. Bohdan tried to use his weight, coupled with his powerful neck and shoulders, to rotate Gibral's large head to the left, where he had more leverage. However, the buffalo's neck was not easily moved. Despite being on the verge of suffocation and experiencing massive blood loss, Gibral remained defiant. He nearly lifted the 700- pound tiger off the ground as he thrashed his head to escape.

Unfortunately for Gibral, Bohdan's canines were imbedded too deeply to be shaken loose. The more Gibral resisted, the deeper Bohdan's fangs sank into his nasal cavity and lower jaw. Having seen enough, Guarrad reluctantly resisted the urge to flee and mustered up enough courage to come to the aid of his brother.

As Guarrad rumbled back to free his sibling, the Nomads were content to remain spectators as they watched the battle continue in utter disbelief. The Nomads had tried for years to dispose of one of the top buffalo in the Guarrad posse, with no success. Now, they could only watch in amazement as a feline, other than a lion, battled two of the most ferocious buffalos alone.

King Sayid was equally astonished but dared not show it. Instead, he redirected his attention to Faraji's recent insubordination and took the opportunity to confirm the courage of his supposed successor—or lack thereof.

Knowing that Faraji had taken a position to his rear, King Sayid turned his head and stated sardonically, "Here is your chance to be king, my cub. Here is your chance to succeed where I have failed."

Sayid then faced forward, with his eyes cast down and to the side. He hoped Faraji would move up into his peripheral vision as a sign of valor but this was not the day for his heir to prove himself.

He contemplated his father's proposal, but whether out of intelligence or fear, he ultimately chose to remain a spectator with the rest of the pride.

Meanwhile, Bohdan's ferocity had taken its toll on his victim. As Gibral's struggles weakened, his main focus was to keep his balance and remain standing. Even in his dire situation, the buffalo instinctively knew that as long as he remained upright, he had a chance of survival. With his neck turned to the breaking point, it was only a matter of time before the big buffalo toppled over and succumbed to the inevitable. Guarrad was not willing to let his brother go down without a fight. He charged full force and just barely missed goring his mark, as his enormous horns and shoulders stirred up a light breeze, rustling the fur on the tiger's back.

Not wanting to give Guarrad another chance to gore him, Bohdan kept a close eye on his attacker and used his huge tail to maneuver his body to evade Guarrad's further attempts to stab him with his deadly horns. Bohdan had complete control over Gibral. As Bohdan moved, so did the buffalo's entire body, making it even harder for Guarrad to obtain a clear target.

Realizing that his assailant was becoming increasingly fatigued with each failed assault, Bohdan seemed to taunt him by waving his tail in a manner that resembled that of a matador's cape. Though exhausted and frustrated, Guarrad was unwavering in his attempt to free his brother for the moment.

Gibral, in contrast, was mere moments away from collapsing. His legs were beginning to buckle while he struggled desperately to maintain his footing in the disturbed soil. Guarrad regrouped and prepared for another attack by kicking back dirt with his front hooves and bobbing his head vigorously.

He sensed that he had one last opportunity to rescue his brother. He aimed his body directly at the target and, with a loud grunt of anger, he closed his eyes and rushed straight forward.

Bohdan also sensed that the end was near as well. He released the tension on his victim slightly and then immediately twisted his neck and shoulders to the left as hard as he could, nearly snapping Gibral's neck and causing the resilient buffalo to topple over on his side.

This caused Guarrad, who was charging blindly, to tumble over Gibral and nearly crush Bohdan under his massive body. Amazingly, Bohdan was unscathed and made sure Gibral was fully defeated by clamping his lethal jaws onto the buffalo's throat.

As Guarrad scrambled to his hooves, he took one last look at his fallen brother and the relentless slayer. Having seen enough, he turned and retreated in the direction from which he and his brother had come.

Chapter XVI
Return to
Crocodile Deep

Exhausted, Bohdan released his hold on Gibral's throat and laid down with his back against the massive body of the slain buffalo. His tail waved up and down randomly as Bohdan stared back at the lions, who were still in the distance.

The lions maintained their positions, stunned into immobility by the intense battle between the buffalo and Bohdan.

The passive stand-off lasted for several minutes, until Bohdan took to his paws. Now rested, but still highly agitated, he issued a warning by discharging a series of ear-piercing growls. Some of the senior sentinels heeded that warning by abandoning their positions and backing away nonchalantly.

Bohdan made it absolutely clear that this would not be a pleasant reunion.

Under normal circumstances, a dominant pride of lions would not allow any intruders to invade their territory without some form of aggression. However, demoralized by Bohdan's display of dominance and superiority, the Nomads uncharacteristically remained silent and restrained. Bohdan began to boldly walk with his legs stiffened in a display of anger, within several meters of the pride.

The Nomads had always believed that their species were so-called "top cats;" a myth that had been passed on for generations. Unfortunately for the Nomads, not only had they just witnessed the extraordinary ability of a superior species of feline. It could also be argued that the Nomads, particularly King Sayid, was responsible for his continued existence.

This omen would haunt the king for years to come and would surely not be forgiven by the pride's seniors any time soon. Had the king vanquished little Bohdan in the beginning, he would still have the reverence of his pride and Malika would still be alive.

On the contrary, letting him live caused the pride to witness the lone destruction of the buffalos, which undoubtedly saved the lives of many Nomads from what was surely to be a deadly assault by the Guarrad brothers.

While these and other conflicting thoughts were shared among King Sayid and the rest of the Nomads, Bohdan all but ignored their presence and continued his trek toward the deadly river known as Crocodile Deep. The sight and smell of the river began to invoke a series of brief, indiscernible flashes of the terrifying events that separated him from his family years ago.

Although he couldn't clearly remember how he arrived there, elements of these brief memories confirmed that he was no stranger to the river's perils. As Bohdan navigated the vinery embankment leading down to the outer edge of the river, a number of massive, strange but familiar reptiles were clustered together awaiting his arrival. Some lay seemingly dormant with their enormous mouths agape, revealing their many teeth, while others appeared to be sleeping.

Undeterred, Bohdan flaunted his own canines and lowered his head and body in a modified stalking posture as he approached the group with caution. Nogard, the leader of these prehistoric monsters, was the first to react to the tiger's intrusion. Entranced by the familiar sight of this striped creature, Nogard slithered and slid his massive body in Bohdan's direction, rolling over unsuspecting crocodiles in his path. He could not believe his eyes. The striped one he spared years ago had returned.

Sage, a younger crocodile, also noticed Bohdan's approach and sought to accompany his leader.

Nogard admonished, "Nogard must go alone!"

Mouth partially ajar, Nogard released a low, extended bellow that immediately caused the rest of the crocodiles to enter the river. Sage, the rebellious one of the group, remained vigilant on the bank with his tail and hind legs partially submerged at the river's outer edge.

Now within a couple of meters of Nogard and still advancing, Bohdan scowled and flattened his ears, while releasing a series of low growls as a warning. When Nogard increased the speed of his advance, Bohdan discharged the full intensity of his roar, stopping the charging crocodile in his tracks. However, Sage, perplexed by the potency of Bohdan's roar, forfeited his stubbornness and began to slowly back up and submerge his entire body into the river. Only his eyes and snout pierced the water's surface.

"Now he joins us," muttered one of the crocodiles, annoyed at Sage's rebellion.

Bohdan and Nogard were now within striking distance and began to circle each other. At nearly four times the length of the tiger, close to three thousand pounds and jaws powerful enough to bite through the thickest of bones, Nogard was without a doubt the most deadly opponent that Bohdan had encountered. Nevertheless, Bohdan's courage was unwavering. Taken aback by this show of audacity and by the peculiar, but familiar, cadence of his growl, Nogard responded with a low rumble.

"Nogard eats all intruders!"

Bohdan continued to circle, changing directions occasionally and making sure to remain clear of Nogard's enormous mouth and massive tail. Too big to follow the tiger's every step, Nogard curtailed his movements to conserve his energy. Once Bohdan maneuvered to the croc's rear, Nogard labored to lift and rotate his huge head in order to keep an eye on the tiger.

Recognizing the croc's limitations and confident that he had the advantage, Bohdan ordered, "Allow me to pass or perish."

The large croc was stunned that Bohdan was able to respond infrasonically and slid back a few meters. Nogard was visibly winded from following Bohdan around. Therefore, he conceded the land and began to creep backwards slowly until his body was almost fully submerged in the river, allowing only his enormous head to stay afloat. Bohdan kept his distance as he followed Nogard to the edge of the river. Nogard then released another series of infrasonic rumbles that were so powerful, the surrounding water rippled and danced off its surface. This was a warning to enemies and other crocs to keep their distance.

Nogard then confronted Bohdan. "You dare to enter Nogard's domain?"

This time, Bohdan did not respond. Instead, he slowly entered the river with his saber-like canines brandished, forcing Nogard to retreat at the pace of his advance. Bohdan was vigilant of the crocodile's every move. With each breath, Bohdan unleashed a low growl to remind Nogard and his contemporaries that he would be a formidable threat. He showed his adeptness in the water by briefly lowering his head beneath the surface to get a quick visual of the other crocodiles' positions.

They continued to hover just beneath the surface, waiting anxiously for their leader to initiate the assault on this rebellious trespasser. This would be their cue to join the carnage.

Unbeknownst to his followers, Nogard had no intention of giving such a signal. The fact that Bohdan had survived the perils of this region reminded Nogard of his own tragic past.

Nearly a century ago, the crocodiles of this region were slaughtered to the brink of extinction by men for their hides. Of the few baby crocodilians to escape this onslaught, Nogard had been the only male. It was because of his survival that the population of crocodiles in Crocodile Deep existed. Nogard had waited for nearly a century to exact revenge on man for what they had done to his family. Not until that fateful night when the men who captured Bohdan found themselves trapped in these perilous waters, had the opportunity for vengeance arisen. For the first time in his life, Nogard felt a sense of contentment, but surprisingly, the overwhelming source of this aberrant emotion derived from his temporary obstruction of man from adversely affecting another species. For all he knew, Bohdan's kind had suffered a similar past at the hands of man and this was his opportunity to show that despite his savage nature, honor and an occasional act of benevolence existed in the wild.

Halfway across the river, Nogard began to deviate from his backward path, potentially allowing Bohdan to cross the deadly river unchallenged.

Unwilling to allow this to happen, Sage defied Nogard and began to zero in on Bohdan's position. Furious at this act of mutiny, Nogard immediately cut off Sage's angle of attack. The rest of the bloodthirsty clan, anxious to sink their teeth into something, followed suit and attacked Sage as though he were the intruder. This altercation allowed Bohdan to swim across the river unscathed.

Once on dry land, Bohdan shook off the excess water from his fur and then began climbing the steep embankment. He did not spend much time trying to understand Nogard's reason for allowing him to navigate Crocodile Deep unchallenged. He had already made up his mind that he was going to cross the river, regardless of the circumstances; an attitude that exemplifies the courage and character of a tiger.

Chapter XVII
Rendezvous
with Destiny

Bohdan's perilous journey to the Amur region was long and took him several weeks to complete. The closer Bohdan got to his destination, the more the cold air engulfed his body like a blanket. His coat had finally grown out evenly, giving him a huskier appearance.

Bohdan was enthralled by the sudden change in temperature and the light snowfall. He had yearned for the chill of the frigid air and the feeling of snow beneath his paws for what seemed like an eternity. Overwhelmed, Bohdan began to flounder and run through the snow like a cub, reminiscent of his early years with his biological parents.

Although the sight, smell and feeling of home evoked great joy, these sensations equally brought great sadness.

As Bohdan ventured deep into the snow-covered forest, he was reminded again of the tragic events that separated him from his parents. He remembered the rage of his father and the love and defiance of his mother as they both risked their lives to save him from the human poachers.

While continuing his expedition, Bohdan found himself gravitating toward a large tree that appeared to have been partially stripped of its bark a number of meters above its base.

With a heavy breeze blowing against his rear, Bohdan felt the sudden urge to sharpen his claws, something he hadn't done since leaving the dense forest of Mortis Bode. As he ground his claws deep into the body of this particular tree, he noticed that another had recently done the same and that those claw marks were slightly higher on the tree trunk.

Still overwhelmed by thoughts of his parents and by the fact that he was finally home, Bohdan ignored the claw marks and continued on his way. Unlike Mortis Bode, which continually teemed with wildlife and often obtrusive sounds of nature, the Amur forest was extremely tranquil, only the faintest of sounds could be heard. As Bohdan wandered aimlessly through the thick snow, his keen sense of hearing detected that the indistinct sound of his softly padded paws crushing the snow was being echoed in the distance. With his ears rotating independent of one another, Bohdan paused in his tracks to determine the direction of this replication.

While he stood motionless for a moment, the snowfall began to thicken and obscured his vision. As Bohdan's eyes pierced through the thick snowflakes to survey the area for signs of movement, he instinctively grasped his disquieting predicament; he was being pursued, but by whom? Flashes of his past began to infiltrate his consciousness with each racing heartbeat. Visions of the strange, two-legged beings responsible for the tragic event that had claimed his parent's years ago had completely eluded his memory until now.

Realizing the potential threat, Bohdan hastily lowered his body to conceal his silhouette. He then skulked slowly through the thick snow on high alert, growling randomly to indicate that he was aware and highly agitated that he was being followed.

Suddenly, Bohdan stopped in his tracks. He glimpsed signs of movement near a snow-covered mass of shrubs in the distance. As Bohdan's emerald eyes scanned the area intently for additional movement to confirm his suspicions, the heavy breeze shifted direction allowing him to pick up additional scents.

Initially the change in the direction of the blustery weather yielded nothing of concern, but as Bohdan continued to sift through the myriad of scents riding the winds, he encountered one that made his tense posture melt like a cube of ice under the blazing heat of the sun.

This brief lapse in concentration was perhaps the biggest mistake Bohdan had made in his young life.

"RRRRRRRROOOOOAAAARRRRRR!!!!"

Before he could gather his bearings, it was all over. Bohdan was blindsided by the most debilitating sound he had ever heard. He had fallen victim to the same incapacitating attack he had levied upon others countless times. This was the sound of unimaginable fear and death that had reigned over this forest for generations. For Bohdan however, this was also the reverberation he'd believed was lost forever; the deafening roar of the mighty Motka, his father.

Motka and Senya, his mother, had survived the tranquilizers embedded in their flesh years ago by the poachers. They had never imagined that they would see their firstborn again. Motka had been stalking Bohdan as soon as he entered his territory. Under normal circumstances, Motka would have confronted any intruder immediately but Bohdan's signature pattern of stripes kept him at bay. Confused, Motka repeatedly muttered silently to himself, *"This can't be. This can't be."*

Only when Motka recognized the unique pattern above Bohdan's eyes was he able to confirm that his long lost son had, by the grace of God, escaped his captors and returned home.

Not taking any chances, with lightning speed, Motka tackled Bohdan into the snow. Bohdan was so overwhelmed by the scent of his family and the unbelievable sound of his father's roar that he did not resist. He was in tiger heaven. Then, as if being mugged by his father were not enough, Senya ecstatically leapt from behind the snowy brush that had initially captured Bohdan's attention. Close behind her were two more tigers, Daina and Boh, his four month-old siblings.

Click!-----POWWW!!! POWWW!!!--------POWWW!!!
Three powerful rifle shots rang out!

The culmination of illegal poaching, trade and the destruction of habitat due to logging and other human intervention have decimated the population of this magnificent species to the precipice of extinction. There are less than 500 Amur tigers in the wild as of 2010. Please get involved in tiger conservation efforts before it's too late.

THE END

In The Shadows

ABOUT THE AUTHOR

Vincent Gibbons is a proud native of Georgia and has lived in the Atlanta area most of his life, while his wife, Sharahnne, is originally from Maryville, Tennessee. They share a love of Christ, SEC Football, exploring their creativity, and wildlife. The happy couple currently resides in Stone Mountain, Georgia with their French Mastiff, Champ.